Spirits *Between the Bays* Series

Volume V

Presence in the Parlor

True Stories
of ghostly encounters
in Delaware, Maryland,
Virginia and New Jersey

Ed Okonowicz

Myst and Lace Publishers, Inc.

Spirits Between the Bays
Volume V
Presence in the Parlor
First Edition

ISBN 0-9643244-7-4

Published by
Myst and Lace Publishers, Inc.
1386 Fair Hill Lane
Elkton, Maryland 21921

Printed in the U.S.A.
by Modern Press

Artwork, Typography and Design
by Kathleen Okonowicz

Dedications

To the guys in the old neighborhood.
Zeek, Smokey Joe, Lexy, Krajak, Carl, Jody,
Walt, Raymond, Bull/Hog and T. K.
You know who you are.
Edziu Okonowicz

To my uncle, Ken Buker, and his wife, Anne,
in honor of their 50th wedding anniversary.
Kathleen Burgoon Okonowicz

Acknowledgments

The author and illustrator appreciate the assistance of those
who have played an important role in this project.

Special thanks are extended to

Ruth Citro, Genevieve Alexander, Elizabeth Kramar, Libby Whayland,
Margaret Lewis, Lori Doyle and MaryAlice McDermott
for their assistance;

and to

John Brennan
Barbara Burgoon
Sue Moncure
Ted Stegura and
Monica Witkowski
for their proofreading and suggestions;

and, of course,

particular appreciation to the ghosts and their hosts.

Also available from
Myst and Lace Publishers, Inc.

*S*pirits *Between the Bays Series*

Volume I
Pulling Back the Curtain
(October, 1994)

Volume II
Opening the Door
(March, 1995)

Volume III
Welcome Inn
(September, 1995)

Volume IV
In the Vestibule
(August, 1996)

Volume V
Presence in the Parlor
(April, 1997)

Stairway over the Brandywine
A Love Story
(February, 1995)

Possessed Possessions
Haunted Antiques, Furniture and Collectibles
(March, 1996)

Table of Contents

Legend and Lore

❖The individuals involved have agreed to allow real names and actual locations to be used in this presentation of their story.

Site is open to the public.

Introduction

Throughout history, the parlor has been the site of many a ghostly tale. Stories of the bizarre, unusual and unexplained are best shared in that formal setting. Terms like "living room" or "rec room" just don't provide the same sense of uneasiness, suspense or horror.

Mention the word "parlor" and images of Victorian decor—with fine draperies, ornate lamps, uncomfortable furniture and expensive antiques—come to mind.

Of course, *Spirits* readers all know that before it became fashionable to use the services of the neighborhood undertaker, cold, rigid, lifeless bodies were prepared at home before being "laid out" in the parlor.

As long as the weather wasn't too hot, the dearly departed's corpse was displayed in its coffin for a final look, then family and friends headed into the kitchen—to raise a glass, discuss better days and try to figure out who might be the next one called home.

Keeping all this in mind, what better place to meet and entertain your guests, and then politely proceed to frighten them out of their wits, than in the parlor?

In this, our fifth volume of the *Spirits Between the Bays* series, we step beyond the Vestibule and gather in the dimly lit, eerie parlor of our very own haunted house. In these pages you will meet new characters, who have shared more chilling true tales from the peninsula, and two original stories of legend and lore.

Among our very interesting cast of new characters are the members of the DeParte family, featured in *The Easter Gathering*, an appropriate seasonal springtime story. But, parent and child readers be warned, there are no jolly egg hunts and smiling chocolate bunnies in this tale. Those who are faint of heart should know

1

that of all the selections in the Spirits series to date, this story is the most gruesome and graphic.

A sorceress appears for the first time in Witch in the Wedge. Some readers will find this quite bothersome, because of all the spirits of the night, witches are the most believable. They exist in human form, in the house next door. Many maintain full-time jobs but secretly perform coven rituals in front of bedroom altars or during private ceremonies in the backyard or in nearby woods.

While a few readers may dismiss the possibility of gliding ghosts—and others may even scoff at snarling snallygasters, roving zombies and salivating vampires—few scoff at the powers of witchcraft.

Historical lore is not ignored, for we revisit the site of the Battle of Cooch's Bridge to report on a spirited Revolutionary soldier. This Colonial warrior seems to have settled in as a self-appointed security guard at a Newark, Delaware, office complex.

Reports from Virginia's Eastern Shore arrive with troubling tales from Tangier Island and other sightings and horrifying events that have taken place throughout Accomack County.

Anyone fascinated in the significance of "dreams" will be amazed—and, perhaps, a bit put off—by the story of a real-life Dream Lady who still lives in Kent County, Maryland.

Events aboard the USS Constellation, the jewel of Baltimore's Inner Harbor, indicate that this historic, floating museum may hold much more than old artifacts and interesting memories.

A report of a troublesome spirit in an old, secluded Eastern Shore parsonage shows that, when the circumstances are right, the haunts have absolutely no hesitation taking up residence right next to the neighborhood church.

For those interested in backyard gardening, don't dig too deeply. Residents of a New Castle County, Delaware, neighborhood are still experiencing the effects of earlier property owners who, apparently, reside below their better homes and gardens.

Don't go Into the Woods if you know what's good for you, and especially into the Pocomoke Forest. Thanks to a tape recording made during a gathering of several of our friends in Salisbury, Maryland, readers will read of mysterious events in the "black water" swamps, woodlands and marshes of Worcester County.

Several mini tales are included in Short Sightings, an addition to our series. These reports are not long enough to be presented as separate chapters, but we believe they are worth sharing. A ghost dog, an annoyance in the attic and a persistent churchgoer also are part of this volume's creepy cast.

Finally, for those who want to plan an adventurous sleepover or break early morning bread at an actual haunted site, there are two worthy bed and breakfast choices: The Richard Woodnutt House in Salem, New Jersey, and Fox Lodge at Lesley Manor in Olde New Castle, Delaware.

Whether you've picked up this book to read in the heat of a summer evening or during the chill of a winter night, sit back and enjoy. Stories of the haunts are not restricted to a specific season. Tales of terror and the supernatural can be shared on calm, summer afternoons or in darkness, during fierce winter storms. Ideally, they're enjoyed best when the candles flicker during howling wind and pelting snow.

If it's possible, read these stories in the parlor.

Those living in an older house should pause and imagine who has been there before.

Look at the spot where your sofa is resting, against the long, smooth, windowless wall. Isn't that where the former owners displayed the dear departed's remains in an old wooden casket?

Stare at the glow on the wall, beside the solitary lamp. Is that slight movement the reflection of the light, or maybe something else, a foreign presence perhaps?

If you're in an apartment, was it a site of violence and anger? Are the bad vibes still floating within the newly painted walls?

Look, over at the window. Is that where, just recently, a stranger, hidden in the outside darkness, watched someone, sitting in the same spot where you are now?

Are you really alone?

Do you too, perhaps, have a *Presence in the Parlor*?

Until we meet again in **Vol. VI, Crying in the Kitchen** and **Possessed Possessions 2: More Haunted Antiques, Furniture and Collectibles**, latch your door, leave the light on and may you always have Happy Hauntings.

—Ed Okonowicz
in Fair Hill, Maryland,
at the northern edge
of the Delmarva Peninsula

Into the Woods

Centuries ago, when the Susquehannock, Lenape and Nanticoke tribes called Delmarva their own, the woods and forests of the peninsula were home to good and evil spirits. When the white man arrived in the 1600s, scouts and soldiers went into the woods—usually during daylight—with both eyes open wide and a finger on the musket trigger.

From the Elk Neck State Park in the north to the deserted barrier islands in the south, mention a forest or shoreline and someone is eager to share a story about its resident ghosts.

Does a large, hairy creature still lurch through Sussex County's Cypress Swamp?

Has anyone seen the black, silent coach—drawn by horses with fiery red eyes—that rides through Blackbird Forest? It makes no sound and disappears in the mist.

Is the "Hookman" still active near the Brandywine Creek State Park? Some say it's an urban legend, but others swear it's the real thing—especially those who have seen the scratches on the trunk lid of their car.

Did you hear the one about the blacksmith and his Lady in White, who ride a ghostly horse near the old covered bridge in Maryland's Fair Hill Preserve?

And when was the last time the mute hermit was spotted in Folly Woods, near Newport, Delaware? It's a well-known fact that the area was a hideaway for escaped maniacs, murderous bandits and, of course, spirits and phantoms.

Have you heard the howling of dogs and hoofbeats of wild ponies as the Ragged Point Man, guardian of buried pirate gold, floats over the sand dunes of Assateague Island?

Many ghost tales and legends are associated with overgrown forests and deserted beaches, and most of the unusual events caused by strange creatures usually occur in the summer months. It's during that season when the brush is thickest, the paths overgrown and the monsters' tracks are hardest to follow.

As new housing developments and shopping centers consume more of Delmarva's coastline, farmland and forests, the creatures of the night move farther away, into the safety of deserted tidal marshes and darkness of the woods. In small groups they meet, cluster and plan. They seem to know that they will be safer and remain undiscovered in state parks and beaches. These protected regions limit both vehicle access and foot traffic and often are off limits to hunters and treasure seekers.

One of Delmarva's most terrifying areas—said to host the most horrible, supernatural creatures—is the Pocomoke Forest. Located in Worcester County, Maryland, southeast of Salisbury, are the Pocomoke State Forest and Pocomoke State Park.

Thousands of acres of rolling woodland and banks of the scenic Pocomoke River shelter more than wildlife.

Old timers recall stories of the days when the river and its banks were used to transport slaves seeking freedom along the Underground Railroad. During the earliest days when settlers arrived, pirates from the Chesapeake sailed up the waterway that American Indians called "black water."

Smugglers, bootleggers and criminals of all types used the trailing vines and dense vegetation of the forest to hide from the authorities.

During the Civil War, both Union and Confederate soldiers lived in secret near the thick brackish water of the cypress swamp and built camps in the woods.

Today, dirt camping trails wind through thousands of acres of forest. Vacationers launch boats and stay overnight in designated campsites. But things still happen in the woods—unexplained and unusual things.

Cat Woman

Ginger seemed uneasy when she talked about the Cat Woman. That was probably because it really happened to her. "It's not a tall tale," she said. "I know about this from first hand, because it happened to me and my sister."

According to Ginger, the events occurred on an old, rickety bridge off a dirt road into the forest just south of Snow Hill. The legend states that you should drive your car, at night, onto the bridge, turn off the engine, beep the horn three times and flash the lights on and off three times.

"We pulled up there," she said, "and didn't think it was going to work. But we were determined to test this thing. I stopped the car, turned off the motor and did the horn and lights three times.

"Then," she said in almost a whisper, "it was real quiet and the next thing I heard was this scratching up against the car. We took off out of there as fast as I could start the car."

However, Ginger was not satisfied to get off easy that night, and besides, she said, she didn't get a look at the Cat Woman. So, three weeks later she went back . . . alone.

"I stopped the car and did the same thing," Ginger said. "I was the only one in the car this time. Now, you have to be sure to close your air vents, or she'll come up into your car. Then I heard the same scratching sound on the side of the door. Next, I saw a faint shadow come crawling up on the hood. I closed my eyes and when I opened them to look, a creature was scratching on the windshield."

Ginger turned the key, trying to start the car. The first time the engine did not respond. It was dead. The second effort was also useless.

Sweating, Ginger pushed her foot against the pedal and turned the key a third time, and the car responded.

"I flew out of there and she dropped off the hood. I never went back again. But I saw her and heard her, and I know Cat Woman is real."

Pocomoke Prom Night

One of the stories about Pocomoke Forest that surfaces every spring is also used as a warning for couples who might think the backroads of the woods are good spots for privacy and romantic moments.

Years ago, two high school seniors left the school dance and drove into the forest on one of the narrow dirt roads. Just past midnight, they were alone in their car, hidden by the darkness of the woods from vehicles passing on the main road .

"The guy heard something outside," said Ginger, "and he got out of the car to check it out. His girlfriend told him not to go, but he said it would be fine. He told her to relax, lock the car door after him and wait. He'd only be a minute.

"Time went by and she started to freak out. Nobody knows how long she waited, but it wasn't an hour or anything like that. In a situation like that, a minute probably seemed like an hour. And the more she waited the worse she got. She was really worried and scared, too."

Eventually, the story goes, the girl heard a scratching on the roof of the car. Something was rubbing against the metal directly above her head.

"So," Ginger said, "she rolled down the side window and put her head out, to see what was causing the noise. That's when she saw her boyfriend's body. His head was cut off. It was gone, but his body was hanging from a tree and his feet were dangling and brushing against the roof of the car. That's what had been making the noise.

"She freaked out and drove off. Nobody knows exactly what happened after that. Some say they went back and found the body. Others say it was gone and his ghost still roams the forest, especially on prom night."

Secret Ceremony

Two young men were walking along a secluded nature trail in Pocomoke Forest late one night. No one knows why they were there, but in an open area they found the outline of a pentagram, drawn into the dirt. At each of the five points there were four or five candles.

"But," Ginger said, "the strange thing that got to them was that the wicks were smoking. It was as if they had just been extinguished. The two guys looked at each other, as if to ask: *Were these just put out?* But, before they could say a word, they were surrounded by about 20 figures wearing black-hooded gowns, like monk's robes."

The two unlucky explorers turned and ran to their truck. Arriving just steps ahead of the band of devil worshippers, they locked the pickup doors and gunned it, spinning gravel along the dirt road.

"They were going about 50 miles an hour," said Ginger, "but they could hear screaming and what sounded like sticks and metal bars hitting the back of the tailgate."

A trail of dust formed a thick cloud in the darkness, and they couldn't see behind them. As the truck drove faster, the passengers still heard the sounds of hands slapping at the back of the truck. Once on the smooth blacktop of the highway, they pushed the truck to top speed and didn't stop until they got to a gas station in Salisbury.

"When the two men got out of the truck," Ginger said, "it was covered with a film of dust, from racing out of the forest. They walked to the back and checked the tailgate for damage. There were scratches and dents across the whole rear and along the back sides. But, what really bothered them were the hand prints that were inside the back bed. The creatures, or whatever they were, had been in the back of the truck. There were marks on the window, right behind their heads.

"Those two boys never went back to Pocomoke again, day or night. I don't blame them," Ginger said. "They say it's eerie back in there, even during the daytime. I know quite a few people who don't like going in there and who swear they never will."

Heavy Bible

One of the best-known tales of the unexplained associated with the Pocomoke area involves a *Holy Bible* that rests, opened, on a stand near a church's altar.

According to newspaper stories and oral history, it is impossible to remove *The Bible* from the old historic church. Anyone who tries to take the Good Book from its proper place and move it out of the house of worship will find they've set about an impossible task. Apparently, the Holy Book gets heavier as it is moved farther from its proper resting place.

"The church used to be located in Pocomoke Forest," Ginger said, "but now it's been moved to Furnace Town, outside Snow Hill. I heard that one guy put *The Bible* in a wheelbarrow. As he got further and further away from the altar, the wheelbarrow got so heavy it broke. Then, when he turned around and decided he'd better return the Good Book back to where it belonged, it got lighter and lighter the closer he went back toward the altar.

"They've moved the church years ago. Since then, some say the spell doesn't work any more. I don't know. All I heard is that *The Bible* still can't be taken out."

Ginger mentioned another story, about a church somewhere over near Cambridge. That site has a similar situation, she said. However, in this particular case, it's said to be a Satanic church and the Satanic Bible can only be removed by one person—the Devil.

What's Under the Ground?

Bernadette, 34, lives in northern New Castle County, Delaware, within a 10-minute drive of more shopping centers, stores and malls than exist in some medium-sized towns. And, apparently, construction is under way to add more outlets so that they will attract more spenders to the First State, "Home of Tax-Free Shopping."

One can only imagine that once, so very long ago, wild game walked the woodlands, flocks of birds descended on quiet, mist-covered ponds and Indian braves hunted game and respected the land. All traces of that past are gone forever, as far as we can tell . . . as far as most of us can see.

Bernadette's two-story colonial is in a development that was built in the late 1950s, when the suburbs were just beginning to become popular. The area was attractive because it offered modern conveniences in a country setting, but it was close enough to drive to the city to work.

She and her family have lived in the house about 10 years, since the mid 1980s.

It was soon after Christmas, in 1986, when she noticed a steady draft of air coming in under the metal trim of the old, original windows in the dining room and kitchen. Later that winter, she and her husband hired a work crew to install modern, replacement windows.

The workers were having a difficult time in the dining room, trying to get one window out of the old wooden frame. Bernadette recalled that there was a tremendous amount of banging and noise.

Suddenly, a glass hurricane lamp—that was sitting on top of the base of a credenza, on the opposite side of the room—flew through the air and crashed to the floor, shattering into hundreds of pieces.

11

"The workmen were shocked," Bernadette said. "They apologized and kept saying that they didn't do it. I knew that. I told them it was okay. It happened clear on the other side of the room, and it didn't just fall off the top and onto the floor. It actually flew across the room. At that moment, I figured that we might have ghosts."

Bernadette said her decision was based on a series of incidents leading up to the flying lamp. Since they had moved in a year before, she had noticed that doors were left open, after she was sure they had been closed. Everyone in the family also had heard noises, mainly banging and rattling that occurred mostly in the kitchen.

"It was almost as if someone was dragging a pan or a glass across the counter," she said. "It could happen during the day or evening. It didn't matter. We'd jump up and go into the kitchen to look, but it would stop.

"There was also the smell of fresh baked bread in the family room. I would get up and look inside of the kitchen oven. Then, we'd go all over the house, thinking there must be wires that are burning, and sniffing for more of the bread smell. Then I wondered: *Do I call the fire company and tell them that I'm smelling bread?*

"But it was so strong, I thought I was crazy. I even went outside to clear my nose and came back in, but it was still there. Sometimes, the smell lasted for days."

In the early 1990s, Bernadette had a Scottish terrier named Rex. She said that breed is known to have a tremendous sense of smell, and that the dogs were originally bred to rid rodents from castles. Sometimes, Rex would freeze and stare at something that was invisible to everyone else in the family. The dog also would go into certain rooms and look around, as if he was checking something out.

"Rex also would stand at the bottom of the stairway," she said, "and stare up at the second floor, following some movement and then he would step out of the way, slowly, and growl, as if somebody was passing by."

In the fall of 1992, after Bernadette had lived in the house about seven years, she came home from the grocery store, holding several bags of food in her arms.

"I looked into the family room and there was an Indian," Bernadette said, "standing right there, looking straight at me. He was there a good three minutes, and I just froze. I stared. He stood. Neither of us moved."

The unexpected encounter made a lasting impression on Bernadette, who memorized the visitor's appearance. As she recalled, he:

- Had a diagonal blue-and-red stripe of paint on both cheeks going toward the bridge of the nose,
- Was wearing moccasins and his legs were bare, except for a leather loincloth,
- Had long black hair that fell to his waist in the rear, and
- Was bare-chested, but he was wearing bone-like jewelry across the front of his body.

Eventually, Bernadette moved to put her bags down on the kitchen table, and when she looked up the Indian was gone.

"As soon as my husband came home, I rushed to tell him about what happened," she said. "When I finished the story, he calmly said, 'I've been meaning to tell you something.' He then said he had been talking to the next door neighbor, who had been having trouble with a sink hole in his backyard for years.

"He was the original owner and had lived in the house since it was built. He said he had this hole and he kept filling it in and it kept sinking. So he kept adding more dirt and rock, and it kept disappearing, like there was a pit of quicksand down there. It was about 5 or 6 feet in diameter, but it was deep, about a 20 foot hole, straight down."

Bernadette's husband said the neighbor started to get worried that a child would fall into the hole and be hurt, so he called the highway department and asked them to go down and take a look at the source of the problem.

When they arrived, they were amazed at the size of the hole and the depth of the depression. They went back to the truck to get a ladder and lowered it down into the hole. All three of them took turns going down to take a look. But the homeowner said when they came back up, they were completely white, as if they'd seen something horrible.

13

"According to my husband, our neighbor said the men pulled the ladder up quickly and headed for the truck, without saying anything at all. When the owner followed them and cornered one of the engineers, the worker said he thought they had stumbled across an Indian burial ground. They found all kinds of artifacts down there—arrowheads, some human remains and an underground stream. They told our neighbor that they wanted to fill it up—quickly and quietly—because they didn't want to get involved in any legal problems.

"Apparently, if they filed a formal report, archaeologists would have to come out to the site and there was the possibility that the house would have to be moved. They said the builder probably found the site when they were excavating and he never told anyone, because he didn't want to hold up the project."

Bernadette said her husband's comments about their neighbor's experience made sense to her. What other reason could there be for an Indian to be standing in her family room?

"So all this time we lived here," she said, "we had been hearing noises made by restless Indian spirits. I have the feeling that they are unhappy with what has happened to their homeland. They also don't seem to like it when we have company or make a lot of loud noise. They react when the kids will holler or scream. That's when you'll hear something smash in the other room. That's when we have the most activity."

Bernadette said they've heard moaning and chanting and there's been the smell of smoke coming from the family room. There also were incidents involving strange knocking at the front door. But when anyone went to respond, no one was there.

"That happens a lot," she said. "Now, when we hear seven distinct knocks, we don't even bother to look. We just say, 'They're playing the door games again!' "

In Bernadette's mind, the family room seems to be a central spot of unusual activity. Often, there's a cold spot that doesn't go away.

"We can even bring down the portable space heater, and the room, particularly that area, will still be freezing cold."

Bernadette said she thinks the Indian spirits are unhappy with the present residents. But, she said, when she's outside working in the garden, she feels a peaceful sensation. "It's like they approve of that, and they want us to take care of the land," she said. "I know it sounds corny, but how do you explain the fact that they seem to become upset whenever they're inside the house?"

The ghostly visits don't follow any schedule or pattern, Bernadette said. Her visitors could be gone a few days and then come back strong, sometimes making noises for up to six or eight hours straight.

"Last week, my husband was so annoyed," she said. "He was in the family room and the noise in the kitchen was so loud that he screamed, 'Please stop it!' And it worked. They were quiet the whole night. I guess I should have done that 10 years ago when it first started.

"I also try talking to them," she added. "I never was afraid of them. I don't think they're harmful. A friend of mine is part Indian, so I told her about the sighting I experienced, when I was carrying the groceries. She looked up the Indian's description I gave her in a book she has and called me back. She said, from the sounds of what I saw and what he was wearing, it looks like he was getting married.

"I was pretty relieved with that explanation. At least he wasn't killing someone in my family room. It could have been worse. My friend also told me to use the 'Welcome' word—Ya-Ta-Hay—that means 'Hello' and it was used by many tribes. I've even noticed the word used in Western movies, as a sign of greeting. So, I've used it as my special greeting when he starts to act up.

"I've gotten used to him now, though. But I really believe we're sitting on top of an Indian burial ground. I also think there are more than one ghost, probably a group of them, because there are so many different things that have happened. I'm not the only one who has heard things. My husband and our three children have noticed some strange events, too.

"But I'm the only one who's ever seen him. I'm not afraid. I've not had any nightmares. I just wish I could see him again. I'd like that a lot."

Aboard the 'USS Constellation'

Some believe the centerpiece of Baltimore's Inner Harbor is the historic frigate the USS *Constellation*, the first commissioned ship of the American Navy. The dark, stately, wooden relic is said to have been built in Baltimore, on the shipyard docks at nearby Fell's Point, in 1797, and she was refitted as a warship in 1853.

Today, the ancient wooden hull and tall white sails that carried iron men across the endless sea serve as an important link to the Baltimore waterfront's past—a time when seedy saloons, dilapidated warehouses and fleabag hotels stood where trendy shops and posh eateries exist today.

In addition to its role as a treasure chest of seafaring memories, the floating museum is also believed to host a batch of ghosts, including former craftsmen and seamen who worked and served on her decks. In a *Baltimore Sun* article in the mid-1950s, a naval officer shared a picture in which he captured a specter racing across the quarterdeck at midnight. That fleeting spirit's blurred image was wearing an early 19th-century style uniform with gold-striped trousers, a cocked hat, heavy gold epaulets and a sword.

At that time, the ship was docked near Fort McHenry, and the newspaper article said sailors at watch on a nearby submarine, the USS *Pike*, reported strange shapes, sightings and noises that were heard and observed escaping from the wooden warship.

According to a section about the city's ghost ship in Dennis William Hauck's *National Directory of Haunted Places*, there are three possible spirits: the sailor in an old naval uniform mentioned above; sailor Neil Harvey, seen on the orlop (lowest) deck; and U.S. Navy Captain Thomas Truxtum.

It appears that Harvey and Truxtum had a unique association. The captain is said to have ordered Harvey's execution, since the latter was found asleep while on watch in 1799. Some might consider the punishment a bit severe for Harvey's ill-timed snooze. Truxtum ordered the sailor strapped to the front of one of the ship's cannons, lit the fuse and a black, iron cannonball blew Harvey's body to pieces with the fragments scattered to the four winds.

But even today, in the high tech age of the World Wide Web, modern tales of phantoms aboard the *Constellation* are still shared, like the story heard several years ago by Sid, currently a student at a Baltimore college.

In the summer of 1993, Sid was training to be a lifeguard at a swim club in Timonium. On that particular night, the swimming trainer was watching Sid and four other students practice drills in the pool.

When the wind blew up suddenly and the sky became very dark, everyone ran into the clubhouse to wait out the thunderstorm. As the sky opened up and fierce sounds of thunder rocked the building, the electricity went out and the group of six was in a pitch black room, lit only by occasional flashes of lightning.

The instructor, who also was a Civil War reenactor with a wide repertoire of interesting experiences, shared what he said was a "true ghost story" with Sid and the other students.

Even though the Inner Harbor is a popular tourist area, Sid said, most people don't think about how deserted it is on the wharf area late at night, especially during the cold, dead darkness of winter. That's the time when invisible old dock workers from years long ago search in vain for the wharves where they used to work and, more importantly, the shot-and-beer joints where they would keep warm downing cheap drinks.

To these lost, wandering souls, the only remaining familiar sight is the *Constellation*, standing silent. Lit by the glow of modern street lights, the ship is a hollow, lifeless skeleton of her majestic and colorful past. Despite its inactive status, some believe tangible relics are able to attract spirits from other, earlier eras. It happens often at Gettysburg National Park in Pennsylvania, Fort Delaware State Park on Pea Patch Island and Fort Lookout State Park at the southern tip of Maryland's Western Shore.

Many of these areas have been restored to look like they did more than a hundred years ago, when major battles or traumatic events occurred. Some say unsettled souls that still wander are attracted to such places, feel at home and, at times, are able to materialize and be seen, if only for a few brief seconds.

Perhaps that's why joggers and bums avoid the dock where the *Constellation* lives. Maybe they're afraid of the remnants of history that might still be aboard and waiting to escape.

In the mid-1980s, the Baltimore City police were called to the Inner Harbor by the caretaker of the Pavilion, a building that houses the fancy shops and restaurants located near the water.

It was about 2 o'clock on a cold, overcast January morning. Apparently, the alarm system on the *Constellation* had been tripped and the waterfront silence was pierced by the incessant wailing of the ship's very loud, repetitive siren.

Two police cars arrived at the dock. After checking out the gift shop, they determined that the alarm had been tripped by someone (or something) entering the ship by the gangplank. But the police would not enter the ship. They were afraid of being ambushed by an armed criminal, and they weren't familiar with the complex layout of the old frigate.

One of the officers radioed for help from a nearby K-9 unit. Within minutes the cars arrived and five vicious, well-trained, German Shepherd police dogs jumped onto the dock. They were full of energy and ready to tear apart anything within their bite.

Pulling their handlers, who were holding onto the leashes, the restless animals were ready for the hunt. The officers led the dogs to the gangplank and turned them loose. Within seconds the five barking police hounds raced up the wooden walkway and disappeared on the upper deck of the ship.

The officers on the dock soon watched the dogs leave the top of the ship and enter the lower decks, disappearing deep into the vacant ship's wooden hull. No more than three minutes passed and the policemen heard a series of horrifying, blood curdling screams.

Focusing on the dark silhouette of the wooden ship, they stared in frozen silence as the terrifying sounds of anguish continued. At first, the police thought their dogs had located the intruder and were tearing him apart. As the police prepared to run up the gangplank, the screams continued. The officers stopped to listen, in an attempt to try to figure out what they were or identify their origin.

Everyone on the scene agreed that the terrifying noises weren't human, but neither were they coming from the dogs.

Soon, two of the five dogs crawled quickly down the gangplank, cowering with their tails down between their legs. When they hit the dock, the dogs picked up speed, passed by their trainers and ran beyond the World Trade Center. They later were found in Little Italy, hiding under a set of steps in the rear yard of a small rowhouse.

Another minute passed and two more of the dogs appeared on the *Constellation's* main deck. Yelping and howling, they jumped off the side of the ship and landed in the cold water of the harbor.

The fifth dog was never found. No one saw it leave the ship. With the dogs gone and one apparently missing, several officers drew their guns, entered the ship and carefully searched for the source of the screaming and the lost dog.

Nothing was found on the ship.

No dog.

No intruder.

No source of the blood-curdling sounds.

The officers at the scene agreed to write up the report as a routine false alarm. They did not detail the bizarre events they all witnessed that January morning. However, no one knows how the K-9 officer explained the loss of his dog.

"My trainer said it was true," Sid said. "He swore it, and I've been to the *Constellation* and, I tell you, I wouldn't doubt it. I will say this, I remember the night I heard the story. Later, in the darkness, when we headed to the parking lot to get into our cars, I was running. I locked the doors as soon as I got in, and I turned on the radio and took off. That was one eerie night."

One might wonder how many tourists in the Inner Harbor have asked:

Are those real lights inside the warship or just my imagination?

Is that creaking the sound of the old wooden hull or hurried invisible footsteps racing across the deck?

Was that a moan?
Did I hear the rattle of chains?
Is that the sound of evil laughter?
Has anyone else heard the flutter of phantom sails or the
clanging of a rusted bell?
Who knows for sure?
Anything is possible.

Author's Note: On November 15, 1996, two tugboats carefully towed the USS *Constellation* away from its Inner Harbor wharf and across Baltimore harbor, to the docks near Fort McHenry. The frigate's leaking hull was corseted in thick rubber sheets that helped hold the ship together. The aging naval floating museum will be repaired over 31 months at a cost of approximately $9 million.

Imagine the ghosts that will be disturbed by workmen, entering dark, secluded, long forgotten resting places in the months and years ahead. There's a very good possibility that more stories will surface along with the ship's spirits.

Look for more information about bizarre events aboard the USS *Constellation* in future volumes.

Tales from Tangier Island

For more than a year and a half, I had been trying to locate true ghost stories from Virginia's Eastern Shore. In the fall of 1996, I hit the equivalent of a ghost-hunter's triple Casper jackpot in the form of a letter from Rachel, 74. She had grown up on Tangier Island, located in the lower Chesapeake Bay. She had lived there for many years before she moved onto the mainland and she had "true stories" galore to tell.

On a windy fall afternoon—with dark clouds cloaking the sky and hard rain hitting against the glass panes in the door—we sat at Rachel's dining room table and talked ghosts. During the two-hour interview, with her attentive grandsons nearby, Rachel shared tales of terror involving floating ghosts, Indian burial grounds and one story of an unfortunate Tangier resident who had been buried alive.

But Rachel also spoke comfortably of the friendly spirit who, she said, had saved her life on more than one occasion.

"I've heard a lot of ghost stories, which are all true," she said, "but that was nothing special on Tangier. There's a lotta ghosts out there, and I do mean a lot."

Rachel said her mother told the story of the burial on Tangier that wasn't supposed to be.

"A young girl died," Rachel said, "but they didn't embalm them in those days. Just washed them up and put them in the parlor. This girl was buried on the side of a farmhouse, in the family plot under a tree in the front yard. Late at night, the lady of the house heard someone crying and carrying on all night long. She said it sounded as if it was coming from the graveyard.

"The next day, the men came over and dug up the girl's body. When they opened the lid of the coffin, they saw she had pulled all her hair out of her head, her fingernails were worn down and

21

the top wood of the inside of the coffin was all scratched up, from where she was trying to get out.

"They buried her alive. Looking back on it, they think she had a sugar diabetes attack and was in a coma, but everyone thought for sure that she was dead. But there was nothing they could do about it. There was no argument that she was dead for sure by the time they dug her up. So, they just sealed her up, nailed the lid back down, and put her back in the ground a second time. She didn't make any more noise after that."

Many ghosts inhabit old houses, Rachel said, because the dead bodies used to be prepared at home, then laid out for a few days in the parlor while the family held the viewing or wake. That's the way they did it on Tangier for hundreds of years. But, in the 1940s, they built a room onto the back of the church. After that, they laid the bodies and caskets out in there.

But the corpses were prepared on Crisfield, she said, at an undertaker parlor in the seaport town. When they were ready for the viewing, the vault and coffin were loaded onto the mail boat and shipped out to the island.

"One time," Rachel said, "I heard about a body they were getting ready on Crisfield. They were in the undertaker's, looking down on him and the body started smoking, from head to toe. They couldn't smell the smoke, just saw it rising up in white misty streaks. He was laying in the casket, and they couldn't stop it either. Nobody ever figured what it was about.

"But even today, with people not being laid out in the house anymore, there's still plenty of spirits roaming around," she said. "We grew up with them. It wasn't anything unusual to talk about ghosts. I don't mind when they play tricks on you and make noises. But I get bothered when I see a form. That's only happened two times in my life, and I'll never forget them."

The first time was when Rachel was 11.

She was walking home from church one winter night. It was dark on Tangier Island. The sky was black, and she, along with her sister and brother, were looking up at the stars.

"Up in the sky, above the field," Rachel recalled, "we saw a man flying, floating in the sky—with no legs. He had a long black coat, with tails and a satin collar. I can still see those tails flapping in the wind. My brother and sister took off and I just froze. My father had to come back to get me and carry me home."

Rachel's second sighting occurred in Exmore, Virginia, while visiting her daughter.

Both she and her daughter saw a man walk across the living room, disappear behind a wall and head toward the dining room.

Rachel jumped up and went to head the intruder off at the other end of the house. Her daughter kept an eye on the area where they had first seen the man.

"I came around the corner," Rachel said, "and I was standing right in front of a man with a gray jogging suit. He had gray hair and his shape sort of faded out below the knees. It was like a fog around his legs. He stood there for a while. My daughter was calling for me from her spot in the other room, but I couldn't answer. I just kept staring at the man. He was tall. I had to look up at him."

When Rachel's son-in-law returned home, they asked him if anyone had died in the house, or if he knew who had owned the property before. After sharing the details of the entire story, Rachel's son-in-law said the description sounded like his father, but he couldn't be sure.

"He told me," said Rachel, "that his father was a farmer and he loved to jog. The old man said when he died he wanted to have a closed casket and to be buried in his gray jogging suit. His casket's buried in a small family farm plot just beside the house. My son-in-law said his father had never been in their new house. He died before it was built, but I guess he found a way to come on in and check it out."

When that story made its way around the family, another relative reported seeing a gray man in a jogging suit standing at the doorway to an old unused farmhouse located on the rear of the property. When the person looked directly at the figure in gray, Rachel said, he just disappeared.

But you don't need to see shapes to know ghosts are around, Rachel explained.

Years later, after leaving the island, Rachel was visiting her sister at her home in Pocomoke City. While talking with her sister about the ghostly incidents they had shared so many years ago, Rachel said a water glass moved across the dining room table. No one touched it. No one pushed the table. No one did anything to cause the movement.

They promptly changed the subject.

On another occasion, at her daughter's home in Exmore, the television in the guest room suddenly went off, but at the same time the light came on. Then, the reverse occurred: the light went off and the television came back on.

When this happened about three or four times, Rachel, who was staying over for a few days, called her daughter into the room. Standing near the doorway, the younger woman watched the sound and light show with her own eyes.

"My daughter was starting to get upset," Rachel said, laughing at the memory, "but I told her not to be frightened, 'cause the ghost was just teasing with me. I never heard of a ghost here or on Tangier hurting me or anybody in my family. They just want to play with you and let you know they're around."

The next day, Rachel went with her daughter to visit the next door neighbor, a 90-year-old woman who had lived in the area for her whole life.

"We asked her if she ever had any problems with lights going on or off and things like that," Rachel said. "She told us it happens all the time. 'It's just the ghosts. Don't pay no attention to them!' is what she told us. Just like I had said to my daughter the night before."

But spirits aren't all mischievous, said Rachel, some are here to help us and make sure we're safe.

In the early 1960s, Rachel's husband, Tom, suffered a severe heart attack and was told he would have less than a year to live. He died seven months later at the age of 39.

"My husband was from Baltimore," Rachel said. "He knew all about the ghosts, especially after hearing my family talk about them back on Tangier. One day, he was sitting next to me. Very calmly, he asked me that if there ever was a way to come back, after he died, would I want him to do that—to come back and visit with me.

"I told him, 'Don't come back and scare me. I don't want to see you.' Then he said that he would come and protect me, and if anything every happened to him, he'd be there to keep an eye on me and the children.

"We had four small children," Rachel said. "Before he died, he told me if they are ever afraid during a storm, from all the thunder and lightning, I should tell them that it's their Daddy bowling up in heaven. And if there's a really big crash, it means he got a strike."

Rachel believes that her husband has kept his word and acts as her guardian angel.

While driving from Exmore toward the Route 13 highway one bright afternoon, Rachel noticed that her front passenger seat was loose and kept sliding back and forth. Annoyed at the noise and the distraction it was creating, she pulled her car off the road, got out, walked around and played with it until she was able to force it back onto its track.

Rachel thought that the event was strange. There was no logical reason for the seat to shift on its own. Someone would have to sit in that chair, disengage the lever and then apply force to cause the seat to move.

But no one was there.

It took no more than five minutes to secure the seat, get back behind the wheel and pull back onto the road.

Five minutes later, she arrived at a main intersection, which was blocked by a major accident. A huge tractor trailer had crossed over the divided roadway and hit three cars. Ambulance sirens could be heard in the distance.

When Rachel checked on the time of the accident, she found it had occurred five minutes before.

"Had I not stopped to fix the seat, I believe I would have been involved in that crash. I sat there and said, 'Tom, you've done it again.' "

Four years ago, Rachel was driving her grandsons to Baltimore. The boy in the front seat suddenly started complaining that his brothers, who were seated in the back, were blowing on his ear.

Rachel was in no mood for nonsense. A truck carrying gigantic logs sticking out the back was directly in front of them. She had difficulty seeing around the overloaded vehicle, and she didn't need aggravation from inside the car as well.

"He told me it felt as cold as ice, like they had an ice cube up against his ear and neck," Rachel said. "But I could see in the rearview mirror that they weren't moving. I didn't know where he was getting that idea.

"We were in Easton, and I saw the McDonald's. I pulled into the parking lot and my grandson kept telling me about the ice and the blowing. But there was no way it made any sense. No one had any ice. No one was close enough to blow on his ear or neck. We finally got things settled down and started out again."

No more than a few miles up the road, Rachel could see the wreckage of cars that had been smashed by the logs that had fallen off the truck. The road was closed from the accident that had occurred within minutes of Rachel's decision to pull into McDonald's.

"I knew it would have been us if Tom hadn't helped me again. It was him stirring up the boys. I know it. I think my husband helped me out again. He said he was always going to protect me, and I feel like he does."

Phantom in the Parsonage

Dear Mr. Okonowicz,

It has taken me over a year to write this letter. I read the article about your ghost stories in a local newspaper back in 1995, but I was still afraid of public opinion.

The Eastern Shore's most haunted house is also one of its best kept secrets. If you can promise me complete anonymity, I will be happy to tell you about it.

Perhaps, after all these years, someone may find an answer—if they will let you investigate.

Sincerely,
Geraldine

The interview took place very soon after I received the letter. We sat in a comfortable home overlooking a river that fed into the nearby Chesapeake Bay. Geraldine is the former wife of Martin, a minister who had traveled Delmarva preaching the gospel at his church and serving the congregations of several others in outlying areas.

The unusual events that were the focus of my interest and the topic of our afternoon conversation had occurred between 1973 and 1975, while Geraldine and Martin were living in the parsonage.

The frame house stood beside a small, white wooden church with a traditional, single steeple. It was located in a quiet, secluded and very tight-lipped Eastern Shore village, within sight of the water.

27

Geraldine recalled her home as having a small, open front porch. It had been built during the turn of the century and rose three floors. Its front yard was small, so the home was relatively close to the lightly traveled street. The building was in no way unique. In fact, it was quite standard looking. A living room, dining room, kitchen, study and back porch were on the street level. Three bedrooms, a sitting room, bath and hall filled the second floor. A large, open attic was the only room on the top level.

There were two stairways, one in the front of the building, between the living room and study. It went as far as the second floor. However, a back stairway went from the basement, through the first floor dining room and into the second floor sitting room. It curved as it progressed into the top floor attic, and it was the only entrance into that level.

Interestingly, on the day she moved in, Geraldine received a clue from the outgoing minister's wife that there might be something unusual about the home.

"I recall, now, that she told me, 'I will not stay here alone.' We were out on the front sidewalk at the time," Geraldine recalled. "They were leaving, and she did not want to stay any longer than necessary. The young girl said she and her husband had stayed in Baltimore during the week and they just came to the church where we were on weekends. They'd arrive Friday nights and leave early on Mondays. The thing was, I never asked her why or what she meant by the statement.

"I assumed that because they had only been married for six months she didn't want to be separated from him. If I had that moment to do over again, I certainly would have asked for more information to determine exactly what she meant."

Geraldine also recalled her impression of the interior of the parsonage the very first time she entered the building.

"I will never forget that moment and my uneasy reaction," she said. "I noticed that the walls were covered with a large number of religious pictures--bad Victoriana is the best way I can describe them. There were numerous unflattering scenes, some of the Last Supper, others with people frozen in different prayerful settings. Some of the pictures were more Catholic oriented, such as a scene of the Blessed Virgin Mary with a large bleeding heart. On the outside of the door to the couple's bedroom was a huge cross. All of it made me feel very ill at ease, and I took all of the scenes down as soon as we moved in."

Later, Geraldine said, several visitors remarked that they were surprised that she had removed all of the religious paintings.

"They seemed very much amazed," she said. "I don't know if they were annoyed that I had done so because I had desecrated the decor, or maybe they were surprised because I unknowingly had pulled down a layer of protection that had been erected against some unseen force that I was ignorant of."

Geraldine explained that her husband was out quite a bit, working in the church, tending the needs of his congregation or visiting other churches, so she spent a considerable amount of time alone.

Of course, it was proper for the women of the community to welcome the new minister and his wife, and this they did. "But after that initial reception," Geraldine said, "the other ladies rarely came to the parsonage alone. They always were in groups of two or more. I didn't notice that at first, but later, after I started hearing sounds and having experiences, I noticed that very rarely did anyone come alone. It happened so infrequently that I could remember the few times it occurred. Also, people seemed to be ill at ease while they were in the house. It wasn't my imagination. That was a fact."

The footsteps came first.

As Geraldine walked from the kitchen, through the dining room and into the living room, she noticed footsteps following her. This, she said, occurred frequently.

"They weren't soft," she said. "They were definite and distinct. The strange thing was there were thick rugs on the floor, but it sounded as if the footsteps were striking a bare, wooden floor. Then, as months passed, I noticed that the footsteps were following me up the stairs."

Geraldine mentioned the sounds to her husband, but Martin told her it was her imagination, the humidity or the creaking and settling of an old house.

"He didn't want to hear about it," she said. "He either ignored the sounds completely or he looked at me as if I was crazy when I mentioned anything odd. So, I stopped talking to him about it and kept everything else that happened to myself."

But the strange events continued. Geraldine noticed that the phantom footsteps would stop whenever she sat down.

Her pet also reacted to the unseen activity.

"Our dog would stare at something invisible as it went by," she said. "It also would never go up the stairs, not the front or the

29

backstairs. But I got used to whoever or whatever it was. As a matter of fact, it never bothered me. I never felt threatened or scared. It was just there, and it was something I had to live with. After all, I was there all alone and we couldn't move. We were assigned to the church."

On the few occasions when there were visitors, Geraldine noticed that the phantom was not pleased.

"One day a lady stopped by to see the minister and Martin was out," she recalled. "I suggested she come in and wait for him. She entered the back kitchen door, and I led her through the dining room. As we walked, the footsteps followed us through the house. We went up the stairs, to have her wait in the sitting room on the second floor, and the footsteps continued to follow close behind."

While the lady was waiting, Geraldine said, the mirrored medicine chest in the second floor bathroom flew open. The visitor saw it happen through the open doorway. Apparently, it bothered her, because she also noticed that there was no one present to make it happen. Immediately, she got up, told Geraldine that she would call back by phone and left very quickly.

"I knew by then that we definitely had something," Geraldine said. "So, I decided to investigate."

Anyone who has seen a movie or read a book about what happens to a newcomer seeking information in a small town can guess the results of Geraldine's efforts.

"All I got was silence and icy stares," she said. "The stares were so icy, that they almost scared you. I tried several tacks. I asked: *Who had owned the property*? *Who had lived there*? *Who built the house*? But I got nowhere. It was hopeless. I could get nothing out of anyone."

At an open house that Geraldine hosted during her first autumn in the church home, one of the guests pointed to the doorway in a corner of the dining room and said, "Oh! This is the staircase!" But as soon as Geraldine asked for more information, the woman drew back and ignored her, acting if she hadn't heard the hostess' question. However, a short time later, one of the women blurted out that someone, or something has pushed her.

"She had been standing in the dining room, near the stairway. When I asked what was the matter, everyone got silent—but no one answered. Obviously," Geraldine recalled with a slight smile, "you can imagine that the conversation and events were not conducive to a Sunday afternoon tea, and the gathering soon ended."

Whenever she walked up the backstairs, Geraldine noticed a definite cold spot at the base of the small landing at the dining room level. She also said that as she took the circular section of the stairway up to the attic she sensed a strong, dark feeling of unhappiness, as if someone was very depressed or very confused.

"As I said," she repeated, "I had decided the place was haunted. But the thing that really bothered me was the lack of information and the apparent inability to get any. I was becoming frustrated, but there was nothing I could do. I couldn't talk to anyone in town about it. My husband wouldn't discuss it. I still find it intriguing that nobody would talk about the house at all. Usually, if you keep poking around enough you'll discover something.

"The only two living beings that agreed there was something strange were me and my dog. Over the next year and a half, I just existed with the silent, heavy-footed spirit. Often, I would analyze the events and review them in my own mind. I'll admit that there even were times when I talked to it. I would tell it to settle down and to quit making noise."

After two years, Martin was transferred to another church. Annoyed that she had not been able to solve the puzzle, Geraldine decided to have a heart-to-heart talk with the phantom. On the night before she was to leave, and while her husband was finishing up some last minute details away from home, Geraldine sat on the top step of the stairs, in the entrance doorway to the attic.

"I really made a mistake," she said, shaking her head as she recalled the events. "We were leaving and I thought that maybe if I talked to the thing it would help. So I tried to have a conversation with it. It was in the fall, and it was already dark outside.

"I said, 'I know you probably don't understand this, but you're dead. You can't stay here. You're upsetting people and it's time that you left.' All the time I was feeling a little idiotic.

"Suddenly, the air seemed to get very thick and very close. I found it difficult to breathe. I was very scared, but, for some reason, I continued talking in the same vein for a short time more. Then I retreated downstairs. Later that night, while I was looking into the mirror and brushing my teeth in the second floor bathroom, the whole medicine chest came flying out of the wall, straight at me, and hit me in the face.

"It was recessed into the wall. There was no way it could fall out. But it didn't fall, it flew across the room and hit me. I ran. I

31

wasn't hurt but I was terrified. My husband wasn't home, and I couldn't call anyone, so I went over and sat alone in the church until he returned. When he arrived, I told him I had been practicing the piano in the church.

"When we got back into the house, he saw the medicine chest. Without a word, he picked it up and shoved it back into the wall. He never commented on it, but that wasn't a surprise. He never would acknowledge anything strange was going on. His church doesn't recognize any type of psychic phenomenon. There's no room for anything like all of this in his doctrine.

"To him, the cold spot was a draft from the basement. The footsteps were my imagination. The old house was just creaking.

"Sometimes, I would hear whispered voices in the night, coming from somewhere. I never could make out what they were saying, but they were there.

"Maybe only I could hear them. I've heard it said that some people are more sensitive to all of this than others. If that's the case, I believe I am.

"I still think about that place," Geraldine continued. "Mainly, I wonder what happened to the person in there. I got the feeling that it was a female, that she had fallen—or been pushed—down the stairs, and her body stopped at the stairway entrance to the dining room.

"Once, when there were two women in the home, I said to one of them, 'Who fell down the staircase?' And one of the ladies, very surprised, asked, 'How did you find out about it?' But before the conversation could continue, the other woman cut in and snapped, 'Nobody ever fell down that staircase.' That's when I knew there was a lot more to the cold spot than a draft, but that was about all the information I could ever get."

More than 20 years have passed since Geraldine lived in the parsonage, but the experiences are as vivid as if they occurred quite recently.

The building is still there. She knows because she has ridden by the church and her old house several times. But she's never knocked on the door, never asked the current residents if they have an invisible, heavy-footed boarder.

"I'd love to go back in there again," she said. "The first thing I would do is walk from the kitchen to the living room to see if the footsteps follow me. Then I'd check out the circular staircase and go into the attic. Maybe the spirit's gone, but if she's there, I wonder if she'd remember me.

"But there's also a part of me that's a bit scared. I remember being terrified there that last night. It was such a feeling of hate and anger. It was almost childlike or tantrum like. In a way, if felt like the rage of a child or a retarded adult, somebody lost or trapped, a very simple person who was very frustrated and angry."

Author's note: During the winter of 1997, I visited the parsonage, hoping to find out if the present residents had witnessed any of the unusual experiences that plagued Geraldine and her former husband. The current lady of the house greeted me cordially and, not surprisingly, she did not offer an enthusiastic reply to my questions of phantom footsteps and cold spots on the back stairs. Our conversation was quite brief and she told me that living in the house "was a blessing," ended the conversation and closed the door.

Later, when I called Geraldine to report on my findings, the former resident asked me if, perhaps, the current occupant had said that the house "had been blessed"?

The Dream Lady

One of the most famous ghost stories is "The Dream House,"
an Irish folktale about a woman who experiences a series of dreams
that predict the future.

When I began storytelling, this was the very first story I
learned, and I have used it many times over the years in programs
for both adults and students. However, I never thought that, one
day, I would meet the Dream Lady in person.

The letter came in the mail, like so many others, commenting on the books in the Spirits series and asking for referrals to psychics, mediums or mentioning there was a story to be shared.

There was one section of this note, however, that grabbed my attention:

"I have always had visions of situations before they happen. I've had several deceased people appear to me, but I don't always know them."

I placed a call and set up an appointment with MaryAnn, who shared her experiences during an afternoon interview. She was 35 at the time, and explained that she saw visions, as if she were watching scenes on TV. The strange experiences started when she was younger, but they became more frequent as she got older.

"Now, it happens about every other week. It's a random thing," she said, "sometimes when I'm sleeping, sometimes when I'm wide awake. I can see something go across my eyes and it can be either persons or situations."

MaryAnn offered an example. Her neighbors had gone to vacation at their winter home in Florida, where they lived for six months each year. She awoke one morning, knowing that something terrible and life-threatening had happened to them.

The next day in town, she met one of her neighbor's relatives at the bank and was told that the husband was diagnosed with prostate cancer and the wife had a stroke and wasn't expected to live.

"I didn't say anything," MaryAnn said, "but it bothered me. I knew it when she told me. I wish I could learn how to use it. I believe it's a gift in the rough. I don't know how to make it so I can help people."

In another instance, MaryAnn and her husband were looking at different properties on the water. One home interested them and they kept walking by and looking in the windows of the deserted house.

They called a real estate agent and arranged an appointment to see the property. The night before the inspection, MaryAnn had a dream about a very attractive, white-haired woman, sitting in a rocking chair.

"I knew her name was Marion, and she showed me the inside of the house, as if I was looking at it frame by frame, like pictures or slides in my dream. It was a very friendly situation. Actually, I found it to be rather exciting. The next morning, I told my husband. I knew I was inside that house.

"The day after the dream, I went to the real estate office, before we went to the house, and I told the agent that I needed to know who Marion is. It turned out that it was the name of the wife of a previous owner."

MaryAnn said the agent was a bit perplexed about her questions, but answered them. The home was vacant, and as soon as she entered she realized that it was exactly as she had seen it in her dream.

"I went around room by room and showed them around," she recalled, "and they were amazed. They just stood back and looked at me. We didn't buy the house. It didn't feel right, and we didn't want to sell our place at the time, but it was an unusual experience."

MaryAnn said her husband doesn't seem to be bothered by her gift, even when she sees visions about people neither of them know.

"I have always known that I lived before," she said, matter of factly. "I often get a sense of déjà vu. We travel a lot, to places where I've never been, but I know what's there. We'll drive through a little town in Vermont, Maine or New Hampshire and I'll say. 'There's a graveyard over there.' Or maybe I can lead the way to a church. It makes your hair stand on end. It usually happens on landmarks, cemeteries or street names. It happens with situations, too."

When MaryAnn worked as a secretary, she was planning to apply for different type of work through a temporary agency.

"I had a dream," she said. "I saw the office, women sitting at their desks. I saw the building. I had no idea what it was all about, but I remembered it."

A week later she found herself looking in the phone book for an employment agency, and she set up an appointment for an interview and test.

"As I approached the address, I realized it was the building I had seen in my dream. I knew where to go. I opened the door and it was the same scene—the office, the desks, the women, the equipment. I knew how it would play out, but I couldn't change anything. I was caught up in the same scene and very upset, because in my dream the keyboard locked up during my test. It did so in reality. The result in the dream was a disaster, and I left with tears running down my cheeks. And in reality, I left with tears running down my cheeks.

"It's like a time machine type thing. It's never been devastating or life threatening . . . yet."

But MaryAnn has seen death—that of other people and their relatives.

While working at a small office, she had a dream about the death of the father of her boss. A few days later, MaryAnn received the frantic phone call and had to transfer the phone message about the emergency.

"I just had chills. I dropped the phone and ran in and told her to pick up the phone. I didn't know it was her father," MaryAnn said, "but I knew it was a very close relative.

"I never told her I knew anything until three years after I had left that job and met her again. When I explained it to her, she thought I was crazy, then she said, 'You're not supposed to know these things.'

"People who find out about what happens to me will say, 'If you know something about me, don't tell me. I don't want to hear it!'"

Having the gift, as some people call it, is not always considered an advantage or a pleasant experience, MaryAnn said. At times it's both bothersome and confusing.

"I just think: W*hy*? Why is this happening to me? Or, here it is happening again. If I could just fine-tune the gift a little, I could probably help people. Sometimes, I kind of laugh about it. I've certainly learned that I have to get to know somebody first before I say anything. Sometimes, I'm actually afraid someone will shout 'You're a witch!' I'm careful to feel them out.

"And, as it gets more serious, I find that I share less. Then, when the death occurs, I don't like to talk about it. I don't think I'm a witch, but I have kept quiet about the gift from some people. Maybe for religious reasons, some don't agree with the power I have, or they think there's something wrong with me because of it.

"My mother has the same power. We've gone to some psychics, and they say she has a blue light in the palm of her hand and she has the power.

"I truly believe this is my gift. I've always had the sense that I was put on this Earth to do something special. It's just that I've yet to figure out what that is."

Get Me to the Church on Time

Many years ago, the secluded marshy fields outside of large cities and small towns were used as Potter's Fields—sites where the poor and destitute, the unidentified and unknown were buried with little ceremony. Other bodies were placed in farm gravesites, in vacant fields and on the edges of woodlands. But no formal records were kept of these unconsecrated hiding places of the dead. Not even simple markers were placed to designate the secret sites of eternal restlessness.

Today, housing developments, shopping centers, fast food restaurants and children's playgrounds may stand atop unmarked graves. Such areas are ripe for unusual events and serve as breeding grounds for unexplained encounters with the souls of those long dead.

One area believed to host pockets of unmarked graveyards is the land located south of Wilmington, Delaware, off the older highways that lead toward the town of New Castle. Perhaps that's why residents of certain neighborhoods have reported an unusually high concentration of eerie occurrences and ghostly sightings.

About 15 years ago, Jennifer was driving through a ranch house development south of Wilmington. She was delivering a document to a business associate. Since the woman she was seeking was not home, Jennifer placed the papers in a slot in the rear door and headed back toward her car.

"It was then I saw an elderly lady, walking with much difficulty. She was taking tiny steps, going nowhere, really. She was quite well dressed, in an old-fashioned, formal fashion. It seemed a little odd, especially for a weekday afternoon."

Jennifer approached the woman and asked where she was going.

"I'm going to church," the older lady replied.

Our Lady of Fatima Church was several blocks away, so Jennifer offered the woman a ride.

"I opened the passenger door," Jennifer recalled, "and I helped her get seated and actually lifted her leg into the car."

When they reached the church, Jennifer walked her passenger from the car to the sidewalk, returned to the car and waited as the older woman slowly went up the steps and reached the church door.

Tugging at the handle, the woman turned and called out, "It's locked!"

Jennifer shouted through the car window, "Wait there! I'll turn the car around and take you to the convent. Maybe they'll let you in!"

But, within the few seconds that it took to move the car into position, the older woman was gone. Disappeared.

Bewildered, Jennifer drove back to her friend's home, thinking the older woman had disappeared into thin air. No one was capable of moving out of sight that quickly.

Fortunately, her friend had returned home and Jennifer described her passenger and what had happened.

"That sounds like Mrs. Taylor," her friend said. "She lived across the street and died six months ago. They found her dressed up and sitting in her parlor. They figured she died on Sunday morning, after getting dressed to go to church."

Jennifer paused, then said, "I remember reaching down and lifting that woman's leg into the car. It was real and warm, as if she were alive. I know I saw her, and I know she was in my car."

For a while, Jennifer sat and said nothing. Then, she added, "I was confused about what happened at first. But as I drove off, I heard a voice say to me, 'Go home, Jennifer, you did your good deed for the day.'

"I believe that I helped that woman get to church, and that I was sent there to help her. Maybe that's what she wanted, and now she can rest in peace. I did feel good about that."

The Dog and the Little Boy

Mary called several times. She wanted to talk to me in her haunted home, before she and her family moved out to a much newer house, and, she stressed, the moving date was approaching rapidly.

The old, one-story, bright blue rancher overlooked Route 40, in Harford County, Maryland. She had spent almost five years in the rented house.

Seated at the kitchen table with "J.J."—also known as Little Johnny—by her side, Mary opened a notebook listing a succession of strange experiences. She said she had started keeping notes about unusual incidents as soon as the activity started, about three years after she moved in.

It was the death of Mary's pet poodle, Bandit, that seemed to kick things off.

"Little things were happening, like noises over the heater vent, or the sound like someone was walking through the bedroom when no one was there," Mary said. "At first you don't really notice. Then, you start to think there's something odd. But you tell yourself it would be crazy to think about ghosts or whatever. Finally, though, it dawned on me that there was something strange going on."

Bandit died in February 1994, at the age of 17, and she took the loss very hard.

"Her death was very tough on me," Mary admitted. "I had her for more than 15 years. She had been a part of me for more than half my life. It was devastating. It was like losing a child."

As soon as Bandit died, Mary took the wicker basket, from the corner of the kitchen where the dog slept, cleaned it and placed it in the attic.

"For the whole week after she died, I could hear the sound of wicker cracking in the kitchen, which was next to my bedroom," Mary said. Pausing, and staring directly at me across the table, she added, "I tell you, I could hear the basket make noises in early morning for a whole week, and the basket wasn't even there. It was in the attic.

"Then, on April 15, 1994, I have it written right here," she said, pointing at the entry, "I saw my dog, Bandit, after she had died. She was laying in my bedroom, next to my dresser. I got up in the night to go to the bathroom, and I actually walked around her. That happened more than once.

"It kind of blew my mind, and I thought: *People are going to think I'm nuts*. My daughter, Roxanne saw her, too, once. That was during the day, through the doorway, while she was playing Nintendo in the living room."

To some, seeing an animal that they knew had died would be an experience they could do without. Mary, however, was pleased that it occurred. She still describes the experience as "satisfying."

"I think because of my grief, Bandit knew I needed to know that she was okay," Mary said. "So, I figure, she came back to show me. I felt better after knowing she was all right. Right after she died, I used to hear her breathing below me, on the side of my bed at night, for a good while. And I liked that."

It was soon after the wicker noises and Bandit's visits that the little boy and old man made their presence known. The ghostly duo mainly used noises, footsteps and, in one instance, something actually said the word "Hi" to 14-year-old Roxanne.

Mary said she was careful not to tell anyone about the unusual things that were happening in her home sweet home.

"I'm crazy enough," she said. "I don't need anybody coming in here and taking my kids away because they think I'm totally nuts."

Her friend Brenda was over at Mary's one day, visiting. Somehow the conversation turned to ghosts and the unexplained.

"Brenda told me about the time her grandfather's ghost punched her father in the face," Mary said. "Brenda's father would cuss Brenda's mother up and down and sideways. They say he even would make up cuss words that didn't even exist. One day, her father was up and about, and he was on a roll, cussin' up a blue streak at his wife. When he just opened the basement door, an invisible fist came out like a shot. It just punched him right smack in the face so hard that he fell down on the floor. He was holding his nose and looking around to see who had done it.

41

"Brenda said he never cussed that woman again," Mary said, smiling. "I started laughing, and then I told her we had ghosts, too."

During the rest of the conversation with Brenda, Mary shared the mumbling voices and the picture that flew out across Roxanne's bedroom. She also talked about the unseen forces that shook the parakeet cage, locked and unlocked house doors and pushed chairs back and forth.

Brenda had a certain level of psychic ability and could do automatic writing. Mary said her friend would let her wrist go limp and allow some unseen force to write messages on the paper. From that they discovered that one of Brenda's resident ghosts was a 50-year-old man and the other was a small, young boy.

One of the spirits apparently was afraid of fire, or didn't like smoke, because it crushed out cigarettes into ashtrays whenever one was left smoldering.

The small boy, who seemed to be about 5 years old, appeared once in the doorway between the kitchen and living room. But it disappeared as soon as Mary started to walk toward it.

Mary said she's heard church music throughout the house, as if a choir was singing, from time to time. But it stops as soon as she enters the room from which it seems to originate.

"Whatever it is, it wants us to be aware that it's here," she said. "I've never been afraid, and nothing has ever tried to hurt us." Mary admitted, however, that she has no idea who the ghosts might be.

"They could have been here a long time," she said. "The dirt's as old as time. The Earth has been here forever. It could be anybody who lived here, or someone who was in the area. When we saw the little boy we couldn't figure out the time period, because he was only here for a few seconds. We couldn't notice anything from the clothing that showed a certain time period.

"I just figure they're comfortable here. They don't know how to get to the light, to be with the Lord. They're trapped here with us."

At times, however, they have become annoyances, and Mary has had to lay down the law and teach them how to act.

"Sometimes they really tick me off," she said, raising her voice to stress that she was serious, but adding a smile to show she was in control. "I say to them, 'This is it! You leave my kids alone!'

"That backed them off for a month or so. Then, the next thing you know, the birds are raising hell back there, and I know that Little Boy is back there agitating them. Then, I yell, 'Leave them damn birds alone!' and it all stops, just as sudden as it started.

42

"You have the power over them. You have to take charge and not be afraid. When you don't, that's when they take over."

Mary paused, shook her head and lowered her voice. "I was afraid at first. Now, I tell them to leave us alone and go about my business. I don't let them run my life. They can only control you through fear."

After several years of living with spirits and finally learning how to control their actions, to a degree, one wonders if Mary will miss her unusual friends when she and her family relocate to their next home.

"The only one I'm going to take with us is Bandit," Mary said. "Bandit's a very comforting presence, and I enjoy having her around. She can come and the rest can stay here. But activity has really slowed down since we started packing the boxes. They know that we're moving.

"To tell you the truth, I'm just afraid that we'll get to the new house and the man who died in there a year ago will be there waiting for us. But, if he's going to be a cool beans type of guy, he can stay. Other than that, he's got to go!"

Author's Note: About a year after they moved into a home in Cecil County, I received a call from Mary. She asked for advice about getting rid of a new troublesome ghost. One evening, her son "J.J." ran into his parent's room, terrified by the sight of a threatening man in his bedroom. Apparently, the family had an unseen visitor waiting for them, or one of their former spirited tenants has taken up residence in their new digs.

I recommended that she place pennies above the window and door-sills. That old Eastern Shore practice is said to keep out the *haints*. She called back and said she had placed the pennies, yelled at the spirits and, following advice offered by a friend, also left *The Bible* open to the 22nd Psalm:

For though I should walk in the midst of the Shadow of Death,
I will fear no evils,
for Thou art with me.
Thy rod and Thy staff;
They have comforted me.

The activity stopped, for now. But who knows how long things will remain calm?

Haunting Hessians

On Oct. 22, 1777, a month after Gen. George Washington's defeat at the Battle of the Brandywine, an American military victory in New Jersey, on the banks of the Delaware River, gave renewed hope to the colonists fighting for independence.

During the 40-minute Battle of Red Bank at Fort Mercer, more than 1,200 Hessian soldiers, under the command of Count Von Donop, attacked the American fortifications. Led by the resourceful Col. Christopher Green, the 600 American defenders defeated the enemy soundly, inflicting more than 500 casualties on the Hessians and British. Only 14 American soldiers died and 23 were wounded.

Because of this victory, which came only five days after the British surrender at Saratoga, New York, the American fighters were recognized by the French as worthy allies and France entered the war against Great Britain.

Today, historic Red Bank Battlefield stretches along the banks of the Delaware River, offering a magnificent view of Philadelphia and the mothballed U.S. Navy ships in the Old Philadelphia Navy Yard.

Open fields, benches along the walkways and clusters of trees complement the granite monuments and old cannonballs that accent the historic site. The public parkland and buildings are maintained by the Gloucester County Parks and Recreation Department and the Board of Chosen Freeholders. But, who looks after the ghosts that are said to roam the ramparts and, in some cases, seem to have taken up residence nearby?

✳   ✳   ✳   ✳

Stella is a 45-year-old, banking professional. Thin, with short dark hair, she speaks with an air of authority and confidence. Her home is not far from the battlefield. If other homes weren't standing in the way, you could see the historic parkland from the wrap-around porch of her attractive, two-story colonial.

It's a beautiful home. She and her husband are the original owners. It was built in the late 1970s, at the same time a dozen other residences were being constructed on lots in a development that now boasts established lawns and tree-lined streets.

Although Stella has lived there for nearly 20 years, it wasn't until about 1988 that the ghosts started appearing to her. "The spirits have been in the house much longer than that," she added. "They probably were there to greet us the first day we moved in."

Her dog, Maggie, immediately knew there was something strange. Stella said her small terrier would growl, jump up and down and then freeze at the base of the stairway—staring and snarling at some unseen presence near the front door.

"One time, the dog was barking and we also heard footsteps," Stella said. "My son was so convinced there was someone else in the house, he took out his Buck hunting knife and carried it with him as he checked every room, closet and hallway. But, just like every time we looked, he found nothing."

The noises continued, doors opened and closed on their own; the smell of the outdoors—like dirt, leaves and damp earth—was often noticeable inside; distinct footsteps were heard moving along the halls and stairs; and, although no one in the family smoked, sometimes the sweet smell of pipe tobacco was in the air.

Eventually, Stella said she realized there might be someone, or something, else in the house.

"Things would disappear," she said. "It would happen at different times, when I was doing ceramics, knitting or even cooking. Items that I was using would be there and then vanish the minute I turned my head. But, not too much later—within minutes or later that same day—the lost item would be right back where I had looked earlier. At first, I thought I was going crazy. Then I started writing things down in a diary. After a few months I reviewed my notes and I knew I wasn't nuts. Strange things were occurring and it was happening regularly."

One afternoon, Stella and her husband were in the kitchen, preparing a thawed turkey for its final journey into the family oven. They both had just turned away from the counter and walked toward the table when, suddenly, they heard a thud.

"The turkey was on the floor," Stella said. "My husband said it probably just slid off the plate. Obviously, he doesn't believe in any of this, but I know that what happened was impossible. There is no way a 24-pound turkey can land three feet from the counter on its own, and the plate it had been sitting on remained on the counter. One of the ghosts tossed it there."

As time passed, mysterious sounds and playful hide-and-seek games progressed to a higher level of the unusual—involving movements and sightings. Most of these activities occurred when Stella was in her bedroom, resting in bed at the hazy stage just before crossing over from the edge of consciousness into the peaceful world of sleep.

"I looked up through half-opened eyes and saw a soldier. He was dressed in a blue uniform jacket with bright gold buttons, and there were red decorations that looked like fringe on his shoulders. It was not distinct," Stella said, "but still clear enough to make out the shape and some features. At first I was scared and I froze, trying not to move and looking at it through slits in my eyes.

"Initially, I thought: *Oh, God! Someone broke into my house!* But just as quickly, the face and body, which was only from the waist up, floated and faded away. It disappeared into the corner, where the wallpaper meets the ceiling."

Stella told her husband about the sighting, but he laughed. He told her she was crazy and made it clear that he didn't want to discuss it any longer.

"After a couple of times of being ridiculed and laughed at about the footsteps and other strange events," she said, "I decided to keep all of my experiences to myself."

The ghosts made their presence known more frequently as time went on.

Seeing them became a common occurrence, especially at night in the second-floor bedrooms. One night, Stella saw two men in uniform—with faces that reminded her of U.S. Grant and Robert E. Lee—staring at her from floating positions just below the bedroom ceiling. They seemed to be studying her, she said. She could see them quite clearly and tried to reduce her breathing and not move.

"When they realized that I had seen them, they faded into the ceiling," she said.

At one point, the sightings occurred several times a week. "After months of this, and realizing that there was no one else in the house, I accepted them for what they were—wandering spirits. I read a lot of books on the unexplained," Stella said, "and I believe there is a lot we don't understand. Just because we don't know about it, or how to deal with something, doesn't mean it's not true or that it doesn't exist.

"All of this area was a woods before the houses were built. I believe there was a battle here, or this lot or development was the site of a sudden death. The spirits may be trapped here and unable to move on, or maybe they just don't want to move on."

Gray and black shadow-like figures move across the walls and ceilings at night, said Stella. They even appear during the day. Stella believes the shadows belong to the spirits that stare at her. However, when they are in their movement mode, their features cannot be seen clearly.

Stella said she understood why her dog, Maggie, would whine and put up such a fuss as the couple left each day for work.

"That poor dog used to stand at the front door and look out the window, begging me not to leave her alone," Stella recalled. "The spirits must have terrified that poor little thing all day long. It would take an hour for Maggie to calm down after we got home from work, the poor little thing. I think all her snarling and barking was her way of trying to protect me from them. But I didn't realize it at the time."

A gold cross hangs around Stella's neck. She explained that she put it on several years ago, on a night the spirits were pulling on her clothes while she was sleeping.

"I was so frightened," she said. "I found the cross in my dresser, tied it around my neck with a piece of thread and I've worn it ever since. That was my first good night's sleep in several days at that time. Today, I have it on a gold chain, and I never take it off."

The religious symbol has been very reassuring when she's had visits from the spirit Stella has named the "Evil Man." She first saw him approaching her from above when she awoke from a deep sleep. His face, in the form of a menacing scowl, came closer and closer. She found the ugly sneer scary and threatening.

"He's been here two or three times," she said. "I could hear him breathing, feel his face on the side of mine. I closed my eyes, held my breath and tried not to turn or look at him, but I know he was there. His presence was definitely evil. He's quite different from the others who have come close and even touched me, ever so lightly, on the top of my head."

Stella said she considers her spirits protectors. Once, while driving with several friends in a car, the vehicle made a sudden

turn and nearly flipped over. All of the other people were screaming and scared to death, but Stella remained calm and knew there
was no danger. She said she owes her relaxed state to her spiritu-
al protectors who travel with her and keep her from harm.

When Stella decided to renovate her home and scraped off all
the wallpaper, her phantoms let their feelings be known.

"We had gotten the old paper off the walls and I was reading in
the family room," she said. "Suddenly, all these shadows were flying
across the room, dozens of them, and I could hear them chattering
with each other, very quickly, making movement and noise.

"I decided that they were upset that I took the wallpaper down
because they used to hide behind it or live inside of it," Stella
said. "I told them that I was going to put it back up and to be
patient, but I could tell they were really annoyed. Well, I did get
the room done, but it took several years. In the meantime, they
slowed down their visits."

Stella said she has heard whispering and sometimes unseen
entities call out her name. "Stella! Can you hear me?" they shout,
usually in the middle of the night. The cries wake her and when
she opens her eyes, Stella can see the shadows floating above her
on the ceiling. On other nights, she said, when she stares up from
her pillow and looks at the ceiling, there's a scene exactly like the
open sky— as if the roof of the house was gone—and you can see
the stars twinkling in the night.

"I think they're trying to communicate with me, but they can't,
and I don't know how to talk to them," she said, a tone of frustration apparent in her voice. "They play jokes on me, and I enjoy it. I
think they like me and they want to attract my attention, to let me
know they're here. I've had music boxes, that are kept inside my
dresser drawers, begin to play entire tunes. They have to be wound
up to work, and, without any reason, they begin to play.

"I've seen pipe, or cigar smoke—and I've smelled it, too—go
up into the air in a curling design, as if someone—some invisible
being—is here, smoking in my house. The smoke pattern is right
in front of me. I can see it with my eyes."

While a next door neighbor was visiting one morning, Stella
asked if the woman had ever had any unusual experiences occur
in her home.

As a result of the neighbor's quick and unsympathetic
response, which included a statement that she doesn't "believe in

that crazy ghost nonsense," Stella decided to drop the conversation. But, she heard that another neighbor was putting in a foundation for a shed and discovered several old muskets in his back yard.

Thinking back on nearly 10 years of experiences with her secretive residents, Stella said, "I was afraid of them in the beginning. I was actually petrified. I thought I was going crazy and losing my mind. I really did. Now it doesn't bother me that they're here. I know they're not going to hurt me. If anything, I really feel comfortable and I always feel safe because they're around. In fact, when they're not active I really miss them. I believe they're trying to protect me, and I look forward to their appearances."

Stella admitted that she speaks to her spirits, letting them know when she is frustrated with their antics and telling them when she is pleased and amused by something they've done.

Has she ever considered having a psychic visit her home?

"It has crossed my mind," she admitted, "but then I kind of talked to them about it and said I wouldn't do that. It was like a promise I made, that I wouldn't let anyone come in here for publicity, or with the cameras and recorders and equipment. I felt like that would be an intrusion.

"I told them you were coming," she admitted, "that their story would be out, but there wouldn't be names or locations or anything to tell exactly where we are. There are a lot of houses around here.

"But I'm not the only one this has happened to. Surely, there have to be other people in this area that have had similar experiences, who also have seen these things. I mean, I do not believe that I am the only person who feels this and sees this. The question is: Will they come out and talk about it? A lot of them are frightened that other people will think they're crazy. Others think if someone finds out, the resale value of their house will go down because it's haunted.

"But, that doesn't bother me, because I would never sell this house. If I won the lottery and got a million dollars, I might get a second home at the shore, but I would never, ever sell my house.

"I feel like I have a responsibility to them. I'm attached to them. I'm attached to who's in here. They've entertained me. I'm not afraid of them, and I feel like I have someone that will always be with me. I feel close to whoever is here."

A Floating Casket
and More

Ivin Tarr, 62, grew up on Virginia's Eastern Shore, in Quimby, and he worked in a number of towns in Accomack County. Although he spent 30 years in the U.S. Army and now lives in Fayetteville, North Carolina, he has family on the shore and still considers the Delmarva Peninsula home.

"My mother used to tell us tales on the front porch of our house," Ivin said, "in the center of town on Main Street in Quimby, near the dock. We spent a good amount of time hearing stories about strange events, unexplained things that gave us the shakes and shivers pretty good sometimes."

On one occasion, back in the early 1920s, Ivin's mother, the late Cedar Marshall Tarr, went with her two friends to set up for a function at the Smith Chapel Church in town. That was when the church used to be on the road leading toward the dock, before it was moved to its present site.

"It was late fall," Ivin said, "the dark of night already upon them as they walked along. When they neared Smith Chapel, they could see the churchyard, but they stopped, startled to see a large, white ball of light, about the size of a basketball, hovering in the air just above ground level in the middle of the yard."

At first, he said, his mother thought it was someone playing a trick on them. But the eerie white glow cast by the ball's light as it came floating directly toward them indicated that nothing human held it.

The three of them rushed back to the edge of the road, expecting the light to come after them, but it hovered back at the spot where they had first seen it.

"One of my mother's friends became hysterical with fright, threatening to faint," Ivin said, "but my mother and her other friend insisted on going back to confront the light once more. As they approached, like before, the ball of light moved toward them quickly, then retreated.

"They had seen enough. The three tripped over each other in their haste to get away, screaming as they ran the rest of the way to the church door. Only then did they glance back to see what had become of the ghostly ball of light. But it had vanished. Disappeared. It was just the empty churchyard, dark and silent."

Ivin said his mother repeated that story about that unexplained incident often through the years.

"As she grew older, senility began creeping in and fogging her mind," he said. "But even up to her death at 93, that encounter with the ghostly ball of light never left her memory. She could recall it in detail that never seemed to vary with each retelling, as if it had happened to her just the night before.

"But my mother never said what she thought it might be, whether it was a ghost or an apparition. She only saw it the one time, but other people have seen the same sort of thing in that same graveyard. They've moved the church to a different site, closer to the road, and there are newer houses built close to the old graveyard now."

One of the best stories Ivin recalled happened around the turn of the century, when a fierce storm hit the barrier islands in the Atlantic Ocean off the Virginia coast. The strange event occurred out past Quimby Point, on either Hog Island or Parramore Island.

There used to be houses out there, Ivin said, before the people moved off the islands and came onto the mainland.

"There are even some of the houses in towns today that used to be out on the barrier islands," he said. "They were brought over here and some of them have some good ghosts that they brought with them.

"This one year there was a nor'easter," Ivin continued. "It was blowing so strong on the islands that it washed the graves away and the coffins went right out into the water.

"This one old casket, it floated right up to the door of this house out on the island. And it's floating on the water, beating—back and forth, back and forth—against the front door of this house. Like it was trying to knock so somebody would let it in.

"When the owners finally opened the door, they saw the floating coffin. When they tied it up and opened the lid, inside was the dead father of the family that lived in that house. He was kind of petrified looking, and they recognized him from his clothes that he was buried in. He washed up right home."

Ivin also remembered an old haunted house not too far from the dock in Quimby. Seems that a well-known caretaker and town character was missing for more than two weeks. He hadn't been seen around town, and nobody could find him. There was no trace, no word, nothing.

Eventually, Ivin said, the people got together and started searching for the missing caretaker. They went through the whole town and looked around on the outskirts, in the marshes and woods.

"Somebody found him in the wine cellar of this big old house," Ivin said. "Seems that he went down there and drank himself to death, sitting on the bottom step. Everybody said they never thought to look down there.

"But the owners, they said they had heard some tapping down there the night before the discovery. But we told them it couldn't have been the caretaker, since he'd been dead down there about three weeks. Even today," Ivin said, "after all these years, they say if you're real quiet, you can still hear him moaning from down there on the bottom cellar steps."

The headless body that floats along the gut near Cat's Point is another local story that has a good share of believers, Ivin said. "It's said that the headless body of a man, laying in an open box floating along and looking for his head is a common sight. Although I've never heard him say it, some swear that they've heard the ghost shout: 'I'm looking for my head!' or 'Has anybody seen my head?'

"Some nights when I was heading home, running as fast as I could at that point between Quimby and Painter, I thought I saw the box out there, floating along in the gut. But I never stayed long enough to check, for they say if you see him you'd better be quick getting away, or he may just settle on taking your head instead. And I made sure I was quick."

Ivin's most intense personal experience with the unusual occurred in a house that stood off the side of the road between Onancock and Tasley. His sister and her family lived there at the time, and it had a reputation for unexplained noises, strange goings-on and maybe even a ghost or two.

"There were a lot of unusual things that would happen there," Ivin said, "like the sound of wind battering against the small wood frame house and curtains flying as if they were being blown from behind, but when you checked there was no wind blowing at all, or hearing the heavy footfalls of someone walking around in a room and talking when you were sure nobody was there."

In the 1950s, when Ivin was about 16, he was babysitting his nephew for the evening.

"The toddler and I were alone in the house, just the two of us all alone, sitting on the sofa playing," Ivin said. "That's when I heard the distinct sound of a chair rocking to and fro, coming from the other room."

As he got up to investigate, Ivin said the stories of the weird happenings in the home had not yet entered his mind. When he opened the door, he saw the rocking chair, standing perfectly still, frozen and motionless.

"I figured there must be a draft of wind causing the chair to rock," Ivin recalled, "for it was very cold in that room. But, I decided to tip the chair over, with the rockers facing up. Then I shut the door and went back to my nephew, who was in the other room."

Less than a minute passed and Ivin heard a blast of wind hit the side of the house and he could hear the sound of the chair rocking again.

"I remember that it sounded as if it was rocking hard, as if someone were really going at it, backward and forward, clanking loudly on the wooden floor. I got up enough nerve to open the door and peek into the room, but I never went back inside. The chair had been righted and it was rocking."

Slamming the door, Ivin returned to the sofa and held onto his nephew for mutual protection until his sister and her husband returned home.

"When they got back, I told them everything that happened," he said. "My sister said, 'Oh! You're just imagining things.' I told her, 'I may be imagining things, but I ain't babysitting no more in this house!' From then on, when they needed me to watch their baby, they brought it to me at my mother's house.

"But nobody has any more trouble like that. My sister's haunted house up near Tasley has since burned down. But that's not the end of the ghosts. There's still plenty of them down there, just ask around."

Ghost in the Attic

Perryville, Maryland, is a small river town, not far from where the Susquehanna River plunges over the Conowingo Dam and starts the formation of the Chesapeake Bay.

On a quiet street, the houses sit side by side, back from the curb and shaded by trees that have grown tall as they witnessed the passing of scores of summers and hundreds of seasons.

It was in a large, older home that had been converted into several apartments, that Janet Adams, her husband and four children lived for more than 10 years in the 1960s.

They occupied the second floor apartment and used the large room and closets on the third floor for storage. On the day they moved in, they chanced to meet the former tenants who were leaving. The woman who was carrying out a box whispered to Janet, "Don't be afraid of the footsteps on the third floor."

That was all she said. It meant nothing to Janet at the time, and she soon forgot about it.

Not too many days later, Janet noticed the sound of walking. It seemed like there were footsteps, coming from above her room and also from out in the hall. But she checked and never found anyone or anything.

Janet's sister lived in the first floor apartment, directly below her, with a husband and child.

"When we went out," Janet recalled, "my sister would hear footsteps in our apartment. When we would come back in, she would say, 'Did you all just get home? I thought you were upstairs.' "

Janet's sister said she heard dishes rattle, doors open and close and someone walking up the stairway that connected the hall between the two apartments.

"But no one came back in while we were gone," Janet said. "and we had been gone half the day."

On one occasion, the two sisters were sitting in the first-floor living room, when they heard a crash occur in the children's room in Janet's second floor apartment. The sisters rushed out the door, raced up the stairs and charged into the room.

All the children were sleeping peacefully.

"It was just another of those things you got used to living with," Janet said.

While Janet's younger, teenage sister was visiting, the girl decided to take an afternoon nap on a couch on the third floor. Janet was hanging clothes in the yard when she heard a scream.

Meeting the younger girl as she rushed out the back door, Janet grabbed her sister and shouted, "What's wrong?"

"I'm not going on that third floor anymore," the girl said, her body trembling.

"Why?"

"Because the closet door kept opening and closing by itself. And the pool balls, on the pool table, were clacking, as if they were hitting each other. But I looked at them and they weren't moving. I'm not ever going up there," the girl said.

"Things like this, they happened off and on the entire time we were there," Janet recalled. "It never bothered anybody, whatever it was. We would talk about it often. We just figured the house was haunted. But we were never really scared. And it wouldn't happen all the time, more randomly. When you would least expect it, sure enough, it would start up again."

Janet's husband was very skeptical about the whole strange business. But that changed somewhat.

"He said he never had noticed anything at all," Janet recalled. "But, one day, he was having a cup of coffee, while he was working on something in the hall. He set it on the steps leading up to the third floor. He said his coffee cup was only there for seconds, on the step right next to him. But when he went to pick the cup up, all the coffee was gone.

"It hadn't been spilled. He hadn't knocked it over. The coffee, it just disappeared. No one ever said that whatever it was in the house drank his coffee. And he never mentioned it again after that, but he was a little more understanding about strange things since that happened."

No one had an explanation about why their house was a haven for the unusual and bizarre. But after Janet talked with other residents in the neighborhood, she came up with a possible answer.

"Word was that a young girl died in the house," she said. "That was the rumor I heard. But, that didn't bother me that much, 'cause when my sister and I grew up in the country, out in southwest Virginia, it wasn't unusual to have things like this happen all the time."

As a child, in the secluded woods more than 60 miles from the largest town, Janet and her sisters would have to amuse themselves with the limited resources at hand.

After their father dug a basement underneath a small section of the house, the girls would go down there to play, take naps, hide out and keep cool in the summer.

"I remember to this day," recalled Janet, "we would go down there, in the cellar and look up at the ceiling. Then, we would stare at these two holes, made from knots that had fallen out from the planks in the floor above. And, eventually, we would see one long blue finger come down through one hole and then one long red finger come down through the other.

"It would happen time and time again. And it went on for several years. We would run up the steps to try to see if we could catch what it was. But there never was anything there. I saw other strange things over the years.

"Like those horse heads sticking out of the kitchen doorway in the old converted school house where our grandma lived. That was some sight that you never forget. We don't know where they came from, but I swear they were there."

Perhaps, Janet suggested, she was just more tuned in to notice unexplained events than were others, including her husband.

"That's the way it is," she said, smiling, "with people who were brought up in the hill country. You never quite get the feel for attracting or noticing strange things out of your system."

Last of the Fightin' Blue Hens?

The open space south of Newark, Delaware, is being con-
sumed at a rapid rate. Farmland is gone. In its place are
wider highways, strings of housing developments, bigger
malls and sprawling corporate centers.

Fields and forests have been topped with acres of asphalt,
and rainwater flows directly into sewers rather than seeping into
the earth and replenishing aquifers. Each year, less and less of the
scenic, open landscape remains, and the peaceful beauty of the
past is only a memory that will never return.

But, occasionally, there are reports of flickers of history that
seem to exist in the shadows.

Exactly 220 years ago, in August of 1777, the Newark area was
the center of a Revolutionary War engagement—the Battle of
Cooch's Bridge. The British, on their way to capture Philadelphia,
landed on the upper banks of the Chesapeake Bay, marched
through northern Maryland and into Delaware, where they were
met by a small group of Colonial regulars and volunteers.

Although the Americans lost, the red blood that stained the
gullies, creek beds and fields belonged to both British Redcoats
and blue-coated Colonial Patriots.

Four black cannons still stand directly in front of the Cooch
House, beside the historical marker on the Old Baltimore Pike.
Lord Cornwallis, the British general, stayed in the historic building prior to his departure to fight the Battle of the Brandywine
that took place in September.

At the intersection of U.S. Route 40 and old Delaware 896 at Glasgow stands the Pencader Presbyterian Church. Historians say it served as a hospital and morgue, where the British took their dead and wounded. That summer, the sleepy Delaware villages experienced a small scale taste of the horrors of war.

It seems, however, that at least one participant in the Battle of Cooch's Bridge still roams . . . restless and lost . . . and, at times, he makes his presence known.

❋   ❋   ❋   ❋

About two miles north of Route 40, on land that long ago was part of the battlefield, stands a sprawling office and industrial complex.

An old farmhouse still exists, but the cornfields now hold different crops: huge buildings that serve as warehouses and others that are divided into much smaller work areas that house business offices offering the services of those in contracting, telemarketing, insurance, medical equipment and building supplies.

Martha is a secretary/computer operator in a busy office in one of the larger buildings. Her company is located in the middle of a series of other small businesses. People enter and leave each day, none suspecting that something they cannot see is watching them.

She got the job at the end of 1995. Her boss and coworkers were pleasant. At 40, she had been around, working for a number of other companies. But, she said, this one seemed to be a good fit. "Things clicked right away," Martha said. "The people were great, it was close to my home in nearby Maryland. I just had a real good feeling about the entire operation."

Just after the New Year, in 1996, Martha was at home, trying to get some work completed that had been backing up. With the Christmas holidays it has been hard to kill it off, so she took the paper files home with her.

"I figured if I could have one quiet night, working with no interruptions, I could catch up. But, when I got into it, I realized there was an important file that I had left at work."

Since it was only a 10-minute drive to the office, Martha jumped in her car and headed east, parking her car near the front office door about 9:30 at night.

"It's eerie out there at night," she said. "It's like a ghost town after five o'clock. There are no cars, no people, no traffic. Everybody disappears.

"I was sitting in the car and thought how deserted it was, no lights, no cars. You can't see anything because it's so dark, and in the distance are the trees from the woods. I wanted to get in and get out quickly. Besides, the quicker I got home, the quicker I would be able to get back into the paperwork and finish. I mean, I wasn't doing it for enjoyment."

Martha unlocked the main door of the suite, passed the reception desk, hit the hall light and headed for the records storeroom at the end of the hall in the rear of the building.

Individual office doors lined both sides of the single, main hallway. As she walked toward the storeroom, Martha noticed that one door on her right was open.

"I had been the last person in the building," she recalled, "and there were no cleaning people coming that night. I thought to myself: I *never leave the doors open, and I shut all of them before I left.*"

Slowing down slightly, Martha reached into the room, grabbing for the handle to pull the door closed.

"That's when I saw him," she said, her voice lowered to a whisper. "I just caught him out of the corner of my eye. I looked, stared at him for a second, quickly turned and continued walking, very quickly, to the storage room. I got what I needed, turned and hurried out.

"I never looked back into that room, never shut the door. Just turned off the lights and went out into the parking lot. Once in my car, I remember sitting there, like I was actually stunned. My mind was in a fog, but swirling and racing. At the same time, the more I thought about it, the more I realized what it was. Then, to be perfectly frank, I said, 'Holy shit!' I was shaking."

Martha locked the car doors, drove home and told her father she had seen a ghost in a doorway in her office.

"He just looked at me and said, 'Okay.' I was talking real fast. Then he told me if someone really was in there and I walked by them two times, I would have been hurt. My mom, she gave me that non-assurance look, like I was really wonking out. But I swear, I saw it."

Later, when she was asked to describe the strange figure, Martha gave a detailed description.

•It was definitely a man.
•The face was indistinguishable and fuzzy.
•He was tall, over six feet high.
•He was in an old-style uniform, and there were two white
    leather straps that criss-crossed his chest.
•His light-colored hair was flowing out, long and scraggly,
    "like he desperately needed a haircut."
•There was nothing in its hands, but the large figure filled the
    doorway.

Reflecting on the strange events of the evening, Martha said a number of thoughts went through her mind. Some were attempts to figure things out, others were in the *what if* category.

"I realized that if it was a real person, I could have been hurt. Then, I wondered if I locked somebody in there and maybe he just froze and was surprised when I came in unexpectedly. I didn't care what it was doing there, I just didn't want it to touch me."

When she went into the office the next day, Martha said she looked all around, expecting to see something, anything, maybe even a spirit suspended from the ceiling.

"I watch too many scary movies," she said, smiling. "To be honest with you, I wasn't in there two minutes before I told the boss, and he said that they knew something was there, but nobody had ever seen it.

"I was mad! I mean, they knew something was roaming around and moving things, but nobody bothered to tell me. That wasn't right. But, the neat thing was that nobody thought I was crazy. Then I remembered arriving in the mornings and yelling at the boss or the other workers for moving stuff on my desk. Apparently, it was our little friend who was moving things. But I felt good because I was the only person who had ever seen the dude."

Some of the other employees admitted hearing footsteps and doors opening and closing. Martha said they would yell at the unseen spirit to stop and go away.

"That was the only time I ever saw him, but," she said, "every time I go by that room I pause and look."

❋   ❋   ❋   ❋

Several months later, in the late summer of 1996, Martha shared her story with someone who worked in a different office in the same building complex.

"Later," Martha said, "I met that person's boss. He said he heard about my ghost and told me to stop over and look at a picture he had on the wall of his office.

"I walked over right away. He led me into a room and this picture was hanging on the wall. The minute I saw it, cold chills, literally, went down my spine. It freaked me out. It was that person. It was the hair. It was the coloring. If I put that face on our friend, it was him standing in the doorway. No question!"

The framed print that caused Martha's reaction featured a soldier from Delaware's Fighting Blue Hen Regiment, commanded by Col. John Haslett. The Revolutionary War soldier, with long, scraggly blond hair, is kneeling near a fire, warming his hands. The uniform is distinctive, with the tall, peaked cap and the two white straps crossing over the soldier's chest.

"One of the women in the room said I turned white," Martha said. "I had to leave. I couldn't look at the picture. I talked to them outside and said it was our ghost who lived a few doors down. But it was the hair that did it. I can't get that out of my head. Reddish blond and sticking out on the sides, like the hat was on his head too long. It was just like in the picture, just like it was when I saw him standing in the room.

"Now, whenever we hear noises in the office, we laugh and say that's just our ghost going for a walk."

Martha admitted she would like to see her "friend" again.

"Every once in a while, I find myself looking for him. I want to see if the person has a face. I guess his spirit is still here. We call him our 'little friend,' but he's big. Since he didn't do anything to me the first time, I'd try to get a good look if I saw him again. I don't know if I'd be able to talk, to say anything to him, but I'd definitely be able to stand and look, at least I hope so."

It was later that Martha learned that the area where her office is located is believed to have been part of the battlefield involved in the Battle of Cooch's Bridge.

"I'm sure there have been disturbed bodies with all the building going on here, and I'm sure the people—or spirits—are unhappy. Maybe this one wants to rest, but he can't get back to where he was happy before they came in here and dug him up."

When one of Martha's friends heard about the event, she rolled her eyes and suggested that Martha take a long vacation.

"I know I'm as sane as the next person," Martha said. "I know something was in that doorway, and no one will ever change my mind. He may never show up again, but he was here.

"I've often been at my desk—before and since it happened—and felt that I should get up and look around the corner, like someone is standing behind me. It's like when you were in school, with the teacher back there, watching. In fact, it still feels that way here."

Author's notes: A few weeks after my on-site interview, I received a telephone call from my friend who had been the original source of this story. He said, "The ghost is mad!" Apparently, Martha's "little friend" increased his activity in the office by moving objects and slamming doors and cabinets. It's even thought to be moving things around in the nearby office where the picture of the Fightin' Blue Hen is on display.

Some of the workers have suggested that the ghost is upset that his presence has been discovered and reported. One can only imagine what will happen after readers share the gist of this story with their friends.

An area historian and friend informed me that Haslett's Delaware Regiment was not involved in the Battle of Cooch's Bridge. But, he said, other colonial units from nearby states wore similar uniform colors and also had tall, pointed headgear. While Martha's ghost may not have been one of Haslett's original Fightin' Blue Hens, its clothing is similar to that worn during the period.

An associated story about the Battle of Cooch's Bridge, "The Headless Horseman of Welsh Tract Church," is featured in *Pulling Back the Curtain*, Vol. I of the Spirits Between the Bays series.

Short Sightings

Trapped in the Shed
Tangier Island, Virginia

Rachel's brother, Bill, had a nice little place for him and his family on Tangier Island, Virginia, out in the Chesapeake Bay. He was a waterman, like most of those who lived on the island, and he was used to hearing about strange things and seeing quite a few unbelievable sights on his own.

"Ghosts were common on Tangier," Rachel said, "but one of the strangest stories I every heard had to do with the shed, out back of his house. But it didn't happen to my brother, it happened to his son."

Bill sent his 10-year-old boy, Little Billy, out behind the house to check on the shed, where they kept all the tools and fishing gear.

It was an old wooden outbuilding, not very big. There was only a single room, with a window on one side and one door at the narrow end. Once you were inside, other than breaking out the window, the door was the only way to get out.

"My nephew went out there," Rachel said, "walked up to the padlock and gave it a good pull, to make sure it was locked. As he turned to walk away, a voice called out to him, but it was from inside the shed."

Rachel said the boy started carrying on a conversation with the voice in the locked building, asking him how he got in there.

The voice kept yelling, "Let me out! Get me outta here!"

Eventually, the boy ran into the house and told his father someone was locked inside the shed. They grabbed the key and ran back to let the captive out.

"My brother was shocked that Little Billy said there was a man inside there, and Bill wanted to find out how he got inside and who he was. But when they unlocked the door, Bill and Little Billy were shocked. 'Cause it wasn't any man inside. It was a black cat that ran out the front door."

Rachel said Bill and his son were so surprised that they immediately ran inside to find the person who had been talking through the locked door. But, no one, nothing living, was inside.

"They looked around for the cat, but it was gone," Rachel said. "They couldn't find anything. Nothing that made any sense. They said they shoulda followed that cat, but it was just too late."

No News is Bad News
Washington, D.C.

In the 1930s, several medical students from a college in Baltimore went to Washington, D.C., to meet with a psychic. She was a famous, well-known medium with a large following due to her worldwide reputation, and she was in great demand.

The young men had waited almost a year for their appointments. That Sunday afternoon, they were both eager and excited about the glimpse into the future they would surely receive.

The medium's practice was to give each of her clients only a number, indicating the date and time of their reserved appointment. This, she said, ensured that she knew absolutely nothing about them before they first met—not even their names.

On the particular afternoon that the students arrived, things were going well—until the last student went into the parlor for his private session. Within minutes, his classmates, who were waiting outside in the hall, heard screaming and arguing. They ran inside the parlor and saw their friend, upset and shouting at the world-famous psychic.

Apparently, the old woman had informed him there was absolutely nothing she could tell him, for, she said, the young man "had no future."

Upset that he had waited so long to get no news, he insulted the lady, slammed the front door and stormed out of the building.

Later that night, on their way back to Baltimore, the students were involved in an automobile accident . . . and the young man, the one "without a future," was the only one killed.

Lady at the Wood Pile
Church Hill, Maryland

Brumfield's father-in-law, Ned, had a little place in Queen Anne's County, not too far from Church Hill, Maryland. He lived out in the woods, in an old farmhouse. Not too big, but big enough for him.

One night, while he was sleeping, Ned heard something. He didn't know what it was, but it woke him up. He went over to the window. The wind was blowing hard, causing a thin branch to beat against the glass.

Down a ways from the house, still in the yard, Ned saw a woman in a long, old-fashioned farm dress. On top of it was a short, white apron. She was holding the material of the apron out in front of her with one hand, so she could gather up wood chips.

Ned watched for some time, as she picked the strips of kindling from the ground around the woodpile and dropped them into her white apron.

She kept at it a while, in the dark, until she had collected a nice-sized bundle.

Brumfield said his father-in-law saw the woman coming towards the house, and he rushed out the bedroom door and stood watching from the head of the stairs.

Then, from the top step of the second floor landing, Ned watched the lady come

65

into the house, right through the closed door. It was almost like a mist, floating in and forming again after she passed through the solid door.

Silently, she moved, gliding over towards the fireplace. Then she stopped and slowly tossed the wood chips into the fire, little by little. . . until they were all gone.

Right after the chips started to burn, she turned, looked up and saw Ned, staring at her . . . and disappeared.

The only thing left behind was the newly formed roaring flames in the fireplace.

"If I heard that story once," Brumfield said, "I heard it at least a hundred times. I believe it and, as far as I know, it happened to my grandfather. 'Cause he told me so."

Activity in the Mansion
Wilmington, Delaware

North of Wilmington, just off Interstate 95, stands Bellevue Mansion. The building was originally built in the style of a Gothic castle in the 1850s by Hanson Robinson, a wealthy Philadelphia wool merchant.

In 1893, the property was purchased by William du Pont Sr., a member of the wealthy Delaware family. Willie du Pont Jr., a colorful, eccentric millionaire who loved horse racing and fox hunting, inherited the estate in 1928.

The castle-like fortress, which now is pale yellow with tall white entrance columns, was transformed by Willie into a replica of Montpelier.

That home of U.S. President James Madison and his wife, Dolley, was, at one time, also owned by Willie's father, and it was where young Willie spent his boyhood.

Stories abound about Willie's unorthodox habits and peculiar interests. Over the years, tales of ghostly phantoms—both human and animal—have been associated with the grounds. Since 1976, the estate has been owned by the state of Delaware and now operates as a public park.

Joggers, horseback riders, landscapers and those who work in the mansion all have reported strange events—from the sound of hoof beats to a ghostly woman in the Horseshoe Garden. They also matter-of-factly speak aloud to the ghost of Willie.

Some mention the lights that turn on in the mansion after hours, noises and footsteps coming from the upper, empty floors. Certain windows, that normally were impossible to budge, fly open with unexplained force.

During a recent visit while performing Halloween programs in the mansion's impressive library, I was treated to two more interesting Bellevue tales of the unexplained. A caterer, who is very familiar with the building since he works with a large number of bridal parties on site throughout the year, noticed his staff standing in a group, looking at something in one of the downstairs rooms.

When he approached the gathering from behind, he saw the focus of their attention—a ghostly couple was dancing in the ballroom. Slowly, apparently in time with the strains of silent music, they glided across the dance floor . . . then, suddenly, the two phantoms disappeared.

None of the staff spoke. They just exchanged glances and went back to their tasks.

Another day, upon arriving into the locked mansion, a staff member heard a motor running in the kitchen. As he entered the large room, swishing sounds pulled him toward the dishwasher.

It was running. But there was no one in the building.

Who could have turned it on? he wondered.

After carefully pressing the "off" switch, the lonely, puzzled staff member opened the dishwasher and found a single place setting—including fine china and silver—being cleaned.

Perhaps Willie had a quiet dinner for one the night before and was cleaning up after himself.

Contact: For information about programs and details about guided tours of Bellevue Mansion, located in Bellevue State Park north of Wilmington, Delaware, call (302) 577-3390.

The Richard Woodnutt House Bed and Breakfast

Donna Robinson, a dispatcher for the Salem City Police Department in southern New Jersey, always wanted to own an inn. She visited the Richard Woodnutt House several times before she made an offer to buy the building during a candlelight tour about five years ago. Today, the three-story brick home located in the center of Salem's historic district operates as a bed and breakfast inn.

But, the former owner did not tell Donna that the structure had an extra that went with the sale—namely, the spirit phantom of Sarah Woodnutt.

As the story goes, at the time she was negotiating with the seller, Donna said the gentleman told her quite a bit about Sarah Woodnutt, daughter of the brick mason who built the third-story addition to the home in 1856.

Sarah was born in the house and grew up there. She was an expert lace maker, known throughout the area for making lace that was used on many weddings gowns. Interestingly, the Quaker maiden never married, but her talents were displayed on the wedding gowns of many other young ladies who did find nuptial bliss.

Sarah died at the young age of 33 in 1889, and she is buried in the Friends Cemetery in Salem.

"The former owner mentioned quite a bit about Sarah," Donna recalled, "and he had a piece of her lace that he said he would sell me. But that didn't work out. I find it interesting that he knew so much about her that he was willing to share. But he didn't mention that she still lived here."

That is what Donna and several friends believe.

The sightings began soon after the inn was opened, in late 1992. People who were visiting from different parts of the country, and who had no connection or reason to make up stories told the innkeeper that there had been a woman standing in their room in the middle of the previous night.

"One of the first to mention a sighting was an actor. He came to me in the morning and asked, 'Do you have a ghost?'

"On another occasion, a male guest was really scared. I recall that he told us he heard footsteps coming up the back stairs. He grabbed a ceremonial sword that we had on display and waited for whatever it was to appear.

"He didn't see anything at that time, but later he saw shadows of a woman passing back and forth down the hall. He eventually closed the door and went to bed."

Donna said the sightings have happened less than a half-dozen times, but during each time the description is the same. It is a young woman in a long, plain cotton gown, with an apron on top. She has brown hair, says nothing and stands still.

"Now, when they ask me about our ghost, I tell them it's Sarah. It's her house. She was born here and died here and for some reason she's never left. The reaction is mixed. Some come back and think it's neat. Others just look at me, smile and say nothing."

After studying the sources and dates of the various Sarah sightings, Donna has discovered a very interesting fact.

"All of the guests who have either seen her or experienced footsteps or sounds related to Sarah," Donna said, "have been males between the ages of 29 and into their early 30s. She seems to have an interest in men of that age. They are the ones who seem to sense her."

Also, if couples in that age range make reservations at the inn, Donna tells them about the resident spirit. Since Sarah does not ignore married men, Donna does not want the wife and husband to be shocked.

"Some of them don't believe me at all," Donna said, "and some just laugh. Some of them look at me like I'm crazy, but at least they've been forewarned."

Donna's son, Earle, and his fiancee, Jennifer, were staying in the Sarah Woodnutt Room, which, at the time, had two single beds. Without warning, the young lady's bed frame literally fell apart. It did not break, Donna said, but it separated into several pieces and fell apart. It was as if someone or something had disassembled it. However, her son, in the same type of bed across the room, was left alone and the piece of furniture remained intact.

One theory, said Donna, is that Sarah does not like women who are with men in the age range that, apparently, is of interest to the building's resident ghost.

Doors have opened and closed under the power of an unseen force. Residents and guests have heard footsteps and rapping on walls. Donna's cat can sense a presence from time to time.

As one might imagine, trying to find good help to work in the inn can be a bit difficult. Fortunately for Donna, coworker Joe Elk, a Salem City police officer, is around to give a helping hand.

Joe said he had painted just about the entire interior of the inn. In early 1996, while working in the house alone, he heard footsteps coming up the rear stairs and thought Donna had come back into the house.

It was so real, and Joe was so sure that someone else was in the house, that when Donna returned home he asked her if the house was haunted.

She replied, "What did you see?"

Then Joe asked, "What was I supposed to see?"

Now, more than a year after the incident, Joe thinks back on it and laughs. "I was the one she didn't inform," he said, shaking his head. "There I was, helping her out and being a friend, and she didn't say anything. But she gives all the guests that pass through a special warning. Then she told me she was going to put a clove of garlic in my pocket and they were going to hang some in my police car."

On another occasion, Joe was painting in the Sarah Woodnutt Room and had his radio tuned into a station. He went outside to his truck to get some equipment. When he returned, the radio dial had been moved to a blank area where there was no transmission being picked up.

"I've gotten the feeling someone else is here," he said. "Sometimes, I'll get a real cold chill. It happened one time when I was painting the inside of a closet. You find yourself stopping and turning and looking around a lot.

"But, to be honest," he said, smiling, "I enjoy working here. I want to see something. Ever since I heard the footsteps I've been waiting to see something. I thought of bringing in a video camera and setting it up to watch the hall, because I know that as soon as I turned away from staring down there, something will happen.

"I even talked to her," he added. "I tell her who I am, why I'm here and that I'm not doing anything that will affect her. If she doesn't like the colors, she can go see Donna. She's the one who picked them out. I'm just here to put them on the walls and leave."

Donna said she consulted a psychic and discussed the events that have happened in the house and the experiences of some of her guests.

"She told me that Sarah always wanted to be a bride, but never had the chance. The psychic said if I could get a piece of her lace and bring it back, the ghost might be satisfied."

But, an authentic piece of Sarah's lace is impossible to find. Some is on display at the Salem County Historical Society and two other known pieces are in private hands.

As an active member of the historical society, Donna has researched her home and the Woodnutt family. She believes that the ghost of Sarah still exists in the inn.

"There's no doubt about it, Sarah likes the men," Donna said. "And she does not like female guests who are with men in the age group I mentioned.

"Activity seems to pick up when we're doing some redecorating," Donna said. "To be honest, I find the whole thing interesting. I wonder why Sarah never married. Why she didn't move from here. I'd like to see her. I never have. I'd like to find out what she wants. I believe she may have lost something here. It might have been a boyfriend. Maybe it was someone her parents didn't approve of. I don't know. I think she knows that I'm not here to do anything that would hurt the house."

More than one person has asked Donna how she feels about having an invisible active resident.

"I'm pleased to be honest," she said. "I think it's neat. I don't have a problem with it. I consider this Sarah's home more than it's mine. She was born and died here, and she didn't get the opportunity to experience a full life. I just don't want her to terrorize my female guests."

Historical notes: John Redman owned and operated a general store in the house in the mid 1700s. In 1856, Richard Woodnutt, a skilled brick mason, built a red brick addition. The inn is located in the center of Salem's historic district. Many homes in the vicinity bear historical markers and are included in open house events and the annual Yuletide Tour.

Features: On the second floor, there are three guest rooms—the Hunt Room, the Sarah Woodnutt Room and the Pumpkin Patch. The Hunt Room is decorated with authentic antique furnishings, including a drum table (1860) and a bed, manufactured in Salem in 1859.

On the first floor, a colonial-era Keeping Room, located beside the modern kitchen, features an attractive brick fireplace. The dining room is used for breakfast and gatherings. The Woodnutt Country Store, overlooking historic Market Street, is filled with antiques, crafts and folk art, and many items are made by area craftspersons and artists.

An attractive cast iron gate, to the left of the front door, leads to the gardens and gazebo in the rear of the inn.

The inn is within walking distance of the Salem County Historical Society. Many of the guests have been visitors who have traveled to the area to do genealogical research at the society.

Sightings: In the Sarah Woodnutt Room and second-floor hallway. Footsteps have been heard on the back stairway, in the second-floor hallway and sitting room and in the area of the Keeping Room on the first floor.

Contact: The Richard Woodnutt House Bed and Breakfast, 29 Market Street, Salem, NJ 08079; telephone (609) 935-4175.

Illustration courtesy of The Richard Woodnutt House Bed and Breakfast

Fox Lodge
at Lesley Manor

As you circle Seventh Street in Historic Olde New Castle, looking for the entrance to Fox Lodge at Lesley Manor, your eyes are drawn to the tower. Its impressive height stands well above everything else in the area, its steep roof pointing like the tip of a sharp spear toward the sky.

Very large, dark carved doors indicate the main entrance. Upon entering, first-time visitors are amazed at the interior hall with its bright wooden floor, thick banister and impressive size.

After a brief tour of the first floor, I was escorted into, most appropriately, a magnificent formal parlor. Seated below 13-foot ceilings, surrounded by massive paintings, ornate woodwork and crown molding, I talked in hushed tones with the inn's owners on a very cold winter night.

Everything was perfect. If a photograph were taken, it could have served as an opening scene from a Gothic, mystery movie. Although the ghosts did not appear during my two-hour visit, rest assured they are there. Owner Elaine Class and her daughter, Lesa Class-Savage, both have seen them, heard them and, on occasion, even felt them.

"The Castle," as it is referred to by the locals, was purchased by William and Elaine Class in early 1994. Since the fall of 1994, Lesa has been in constant residence at the site, doing much of the plastering and painting of the 142-year-old mansion that has more than 40 rooms.

The owners believe the ghost—or at least one of the most active spirits—is that of Jane Lesley, wife of Dr. Allen Vorhees Lesley who had ordered the mansion built. But the doctor also appears from time to time.

73

Lesa, who lives in one of the several apartments that have been built into the main house and in the carriage house on the property, has spent many hours in the mansion. She does a large part of the reconstruction and renovations with her mother, who is in charge of the project.

"The first question people ask when they come inside is," she said, " 'Is this place haunted?' and I answer, 'Yes!' They don't expect you to say 'Yes.' When they hear your answer, they usually have this frozen smile, and they don't say anything. They're speechless at that point."

The local people, added Elaine, who manages and operates the inn, aren't as surprised when there's talk of footsteps in the night. Elaine said more than a few of the area residents have asked her if she's seen any ghosts.

"No one can tell you anything specific," Elaine said. "But a lot of people have said something has happened up in the tower and also down in the basement. But we haven't found out what."

Soon after purchasing the property, Elaine's mother came to live with her on the site for about five weeks. The building was totally empty. There was no furniture, and many repairs had to be made.

Elaine's mother said she had a dream about a Navy or Air Force captain with a blue cape. He was standing in the gardens on the side of the house. She saw the figure look up at the windows, bow and run down the outside stairs into the basement. Elaine and her mother laughed about the dream and tried to figure out what it could mean.

A few weeks later, while workmen were carrying boxes of papers and books out of the building, a book fell onto the floor and hit Elaine's mother's foot. As she bent over to pick it up, she noticed it was a pilot's log. Eventually, the new owners found out that many rooms in the mansion had been rented to pilots.

Not particularly believing it to be a coincidence, Elaine said she thinks that the first incident involved a spirit who came to her mother in a dream, and the pilot may be one of the building's resident ghosts.

Later, while sanding walls and floors in the seven-room, third-floor apartment, Lesa saw a shadow out of the corner of her eye. Thinking her mother had come home, she stopped her work, looked and found that she was alone.

Soon, the shadowy movement occurred again. Then she clearly heard the sound of a woman laughing.

"I got scared then," Lesa said. "I had the distinct impression, the feeling that there was a woman and that it was important or urgent that I leave. Actually," Lesa said, smiling, "it was about six o'clock, and I felt whoever it was wanted the apartment back by six o'clock. So I left."

A week later, Elaine and Lesa both were working in the same apartment. At six o'clock, Lesa again got the feeling that it was time to leave. She told her mother, who started laughing and asked aloud, "What are they going to do?"

Suddenly, Elaine started shouting for Lesa to leave very quickly and get down the steps.

Her daughter was confused and asked why there was such a rush.

Elaine explained, "I was up at the top of the stairs and I felt hands on my back, pushing me slightly—not dangerously, but they were definitely there. I had goose bumps. I felt there were six males and one female and that they were all rushing toward me to get me to go down the stairway."

Smiling at her mother across the table, Lesa said, "Never again, did we work past six o'clock in the third floor apartment."

It was also in the third floor apartment that Lesa and her mother have heard conversations—not indistinct murmurs, but clearly spoken sentences.

Once, while they were at opposite ends of the apartment, they both heard someone say: "It's looking really good up here. It really is." When Lesa and Elaine both turned, they asked if the other one had spoken. Neither woman had said a word. But they both repeated the sentence that they each had just heard.

Elaine said she's noticed that workers who are hired for short projects are uncomfortable in the building and they want to get their work done and get out quickly.

"But," Elaine said, "I've never been afraid and have never felt threatened here. I almost feel protected or watched out for. I think it's fun."

Lesa agreed. "In the beginning, you're frightened or bothered by the initial shock that something is happening. At first, it catches you off guard. But you get used to it."

One evening Elaine and Lesa saw a woman looking into the house through a window on the first-floor back stairway. When they compared what they had seen, they agreed it was the same woman—fairly young and smiling.

In Lesa's bedroom, both she and her mother have seen a man, dressed totally in white, seated near the fireplace with his legs crossed and staring straight ahead.

After investigating the history of the house, the current owners discovered that Lesa's room was Dr. Allen Vorhees Lesley's examination room where he served his patients.

Unexplained and sudden movement by shadowy figures is something that both Elaine and Lesa said they have grown to accept and expect.

Elaine described the phantoms as, "Not just wispy, like a cloud, but actually having the form of a human being. It would be like seeing a motion, or seeing you, out of the corner of my eye as you passed by rapidly. Both of my cats are aware that there is something else here in the house. At times, they'll freeze and they'll stare at an area where they must see some motion or something moving."

But even innkeepers who have grown accustomed to foggy shapes can get too much of a good thing.

"I was here by myself," Lesa recalled, "while my mom was in California. I got tired of the noise and the movement. So I told them that, "I don't need this right now!' And they stayed away for six months. Actually, I started to miss them and I asked them to come back and said I was sorry. We seem to see them more in the winter than in the summer, but then we're inside more during that time of the year."

Some believe that the most interesting stories are related to the incidents with the pennies.

Lesa explained that as she prepares each room for repair and renovation, every portion of the ceiling, walls and floor are scraped, cleaned, vacuumed and dusted. Then, huge canvas tarps are laid down before any work begins.

When she completed her plaster work and painting in the first room of the infamous third-floor apartment, Lesa began cleaning things up and discovered a penny, lying in the center of the room, under the tarp.

"I picked it up," she said, "and I remember wondering how it got there, because I had cleaned that place from top to bottom. I looked at the date. There was nothing significant, it was just a regular penny. I put it in my pocket and didn't say anything about it. But I thought it was weird because it shouldn't have been there.

"Then, when I did the second room and started cleaning it up, the same thing happened. Another penny was in the center of the room. Now, I recalled using the vacuum cleaner in all the corners and getting the dirt and dust up from between the slats in the floorboards, from under the radiators, and from the inside corners of the closets. I would have seen the penny or cleaned it up if it was there when I started."

Elaine added that when they finished every room in that apartment, they always found a single penny in the center of the floor, and she couldn't figure out how any other person could have been involved. No one could be playing a trick because no one else had access to the building.

A local real estate agent provided a partial answer to the mystery. He gave Elaine a magazine article about "Penny Ghosts," which stated that during the Victorian period people would place pennies over door and window sills to keep ghosts and spirits out and stop them from entering a home.

"To me the pennies were a signal," said Elaine. "It was like the ghosts were saying, 'Ha! You can't keep us out.' "

Lesa added, "To me, it was their way of saying good luck with the renovation."

Elaine said that much later she also found a penny in the Jane Lesley Room after her very first guests had left. The owner recalled that she was very careful to take special care in cleaning up the room. When she returned after making the bed and vacuuming the floor, there was a penny—with the head facing up—in the middle of the large area rug in the middle of the room.

"I think it's Jane," said Elaine. "It's her way of saying that she is glad the house has life again and that she approves of what we are doing. I love it here, because architecturally it's beautiful and I'm glad we're able to save a structure such as this.

"I've had people who have come here say they like how the house feels. It's a healing house. People come here and they get a sense of comfort and healing, and they leave feeling good.

"When you're sitting here alone, working or reading within these walls, you can forget about the outside world and almost feel like you're back in another time."

Historical notes: The three-story structure, which includes an impressive tower, was built in 1855 and is an authentic example of Gothic Revival architecture. The building's highest point offers a spectacular view of New Castle and the Delaware River. The building—which has more than 40 rooms—retains much of the original elements and decorative features. It is listed on the National Register of Historic Buildings. The structure had been built as a doctor's office and residence. Later, it was the site of a town newspaper. For a 15-year period in the late 1800s it was vacant and watched over by a solitary caretaker.

Secret rooms were included in the mansion's original plans. Because of those hidden areas and a tunnel that led from the basement to the river, some believe the building was a stop along the Underground Railway.

According to one legend, two skeletons were found in a closet on the second floor when the building was reopened after being vacant for 15 years. The wrists of the two skeletons were shackled together, and some have suggested that they were escaped prisoners from a nearby town jail who hid themselves a little too well in the empty mansion.

Features: There are three guest rooms—Jane's Room, Malveen's Room and Lesa's Room—each with a radio and a private bath. The absence of room telephones and televisions ensures a quiet, uninterrupted stay and adds to the historic charm during the visit. Tasty, out-of-the-ordinary breakfast fare is served in the dining room. A Victorian and medieval-style outdoor garden surrounds the home and offers visitors a place to relax and stroll. High ceilings, ornately carved banisters and fireplace mantles and an impressive entry hall add to "The Castle's" Old World charm.

Sightings: In the third-floor private apartment and in the owner's second-floor private quarters. Near the first-floor window on the back stairway. On the first-floor landing of the main stairway. In the gardens, throughout the first-floor parlor and in the watchman's room, beside the entry foyer.

Contact: Fox Lodge at Lesley Manor, 123 West Seventh Street, New Castle, DE 19720; telephone (302) 328-0768.

Illustration courtesy of Fox Lodge at Lesley Manor

Witch in the Wedge

H er name is Melinda. That's what people say, anyway. No one has ever talked to her, or even gotten close, as far as I know. She's been there forever, up in the forests of the White Clay Creek Preserve, off Hopkins Road, just north of Newark, on the border where the states of Delaware, Maryland and Pennsylvania meet.

It's a strange area they call The Wedge. For hundreds of years, until 1921, it wasn't certain which state owned the no-man's-land, pie-shaped triangle. Moonshiners, bandits, gamblers, a few murderers and assorted small time outlaws lived in log cabins and shacks, dividing up their loot and ignoring the law from the three surrounding states.

No one wanted to go into The Wedge, not even the police.

Too many who had wandered into its forests and gullies didn't come out. Hunters never made it home. Travelers who tried to take the shortcut never arrived at their destinations. Children who wandered off, ignoring their parents' warnings, became the "lost children" of The Wedge.

When that happened, the old folks would whisper the name *Melinda.*

"It's the work of the Witch of The Wedge," or "I hear she got herself another one," they'd say.

It is impossible to find out the origin of Melinda's existence. Folklore files in the local libraries, old newspaper editions and area history books make passing reference to disappearances in The Wedge, but there is no specific mention of Melinda.

After interviews with several old timers, those few who would talk at all, three possible explanations were discovered about how Melinda may have come to be:

•She had been a young girl waiting for her fiancee, who went off to the Civil War, but he returned with a new bride. Broken hearted and embarrassed, Melinda, who was from an old Newark family, ran off into the woods north of town and never came home.

•While traveling at night along a shortcut through The Wedge, a woman was stopped by robbers. After beating her and disfiguring her face, they left her on the road to die. Her horse arrived home, but she did not. Out of her mind, she was saved by the animals and lives with them to this day.

•An Elkton farmer, who was known to beat his children badly, threw his oldest daughter Melinda out of the house, but not before he hit her face with a hot fireplace poker. Scarred for life, she dared not go into town and ran off to live by herself in The Wedge.

While none of these stories can be confirmed, in the 1890s there were reports of an old woman, dressed in a tattered black cape. Spotted infrequently at the edge of the forest picking berries, she was seen traveling in the company of animals. When approached or called to, she disappeared into the brush.

Tales of the Witch of The Wedge continued over the years.

At the turn of the century, several trespassers into the thick woods disappeared, especially those who went in alone, and definitely anyone who was stupid enough to enter the woods of The Wedge at night.

When fishermen along the White Clay Creek would not return, their boots were found at the spot they were last seen, but no other clue to their whereabouts was discovered.

No tracks leading away. No trails or broken brush.

Absolutely no clues. Nothing.

Anyone separated from his mates in the search parties that followed would experience a similar fate.

Again, only a pair of empty boots or shoes was left behind. Folks figured these were warnings for others not to come any farther.

Even children were not spared.

In the 1920s, a gang of young boys thought a midnight search for Melinda would be proper initiation for new members wanting to join their club. Within an hour of their trip into The Wedge, three of the seven gang members disappeared.

A few days later, three pairs of tiny shoes were found near the creekbed, close to where it now meets the bridge on Hopkins Road.

The club disbanded quickly, due to lack of membership.

To no one's surprise, trips into the dense brush of The Wedge ceased for many years. Even police, parents and officials declined to pursue the search for any of the missing.

"Only a damn fool would go out there, anyway," locals said. "You're certain to be lookin' for trouble out there for sure."

"Let the old buzzard be," other folks said. "She don't bother nobody unless they go into there lookin' after her. Besides, what's the place good for anyway? Just a lot of brush and brambles. If she wants to live out there with them animals, just leave the old gal be."

And people did. Until a rumor of buried treasure swept the area.

It seems a drunk named Reds was having quite a few too many at the Deer Park Tavern in Newark. Late one summer night, he claimed that a chest full of gold, hidden by a moonshiner who had just died, was buried under an old oak tree with three broken limbs.

Reds swore he could show the way, knew the spot where the treasure chest was waiting to be dug up. But he needed a few brave volunteers for protection from the Witch in The Wedge.

Now this was in the 1930s, during the Depression, and two things were in Reds' favor: People were very poor and would do anything for money, and some folks were starting to think that all this talk about ghosts and witches in The Wedge was a lot of bunk—old wives' tales to scare little children and nothing more.

What kind of a grown man would be afraid of this nonsense? Besides, no one had ever seen this so-called Melinda.

Two dozen grown men with guns and large dogs set out north of town—going for the gold.

Early in the morning they parked their beat up pickups off the road and tied their horses to the tree branches hanging along the creek.

A dozen bloodhounds and hunting dogs came along for protection and tracking purposes. The animals were excited, sniffing at every tree and stump.

The hot morning headed toward a hotter afternoon, and still Reds could not find the old oak that marked the spot. Several times he pointed to "the spot," and several times the group dug, but the result was the same—dirt, tree roots and frustration.

The summer humidity and heat became unbearable, and even the dogs were wearing out.

Dusk arrived, and the search party faced a good two-hour hike back to the vehicles and horses. Some wanted to give it up, but just as many others wanted to continue.

The quitters realized that, if they gave up the search, those who remained might find the gold without them. They all agreed to push on.

Confused and under a lot of pressure, Reds sat down and took a healthy swig from a half-pint of bar whiskey he had brought along for comfort in a tough situation.

They decided there were enough lanterns for light, so into the dark forest they trudged. The moon was full, and Reds swore he could make out the treasure spot by looking at the tops of the trees.

Four more times Reds pointed to the spot.

Four more times they dug and came up empty.

Tempers were short. Arguments began. Punches were thrown.

Suddenly, at 2:30 in the morning, deep in the eerie woods of The Wedge, they all stopped. Startled by the cackle, the shrill laughter, of a crazed being that screeched out a sound that turned their blood to ice water.

"Get out of my woods!" the voice commanded.

It was repeated a half-dozen times, and seemed to come from every direction. Surrounded and nervous, one of the hunters pulled a trigger. His gunshot blast lit up the brush.

Others followed. Shots aimed at nothing, offering only noise and more confusion. Then, total silence cut through the drifting smoke of their guns.

Again the shrill warning: *"Leave my woods or you'll all die!"*

No one moved this time. The huge German Shepherds and full grown bloodhounds were crying, whimpering like puppies.

Then, dropping out of the trees, like hundreds of heavy raindrops in a freak thunderstorm, were squirrels and opossum, snakes and raccoons, large bugs and spiders, scratching the backs, hair and heads of the hunters. As the creatures hit the ground, they nipped at the intruders' feet.

Throwing down their guns and lanterns, the treasure seekers fled into the darkness, running into trees and tripping over exposed limbs. Their faces were ripped by thorn bushes, their bodies pushed and beaten by unseen forces.

A herd of large deer ran by, adding confusion to the retreat.

In the hunters' race toward safety, most were separated from the group. Many spent the rest of the night hovering beneath wicked looking trees and praying they would live to see the dawn.

Slowly, alone and in two's and three's, the humiliated treasure hunters reached the road that had served as their starting point. But the horses were gone and the trucks had been overturned. Tires were punctured, windshields broken.

Of the 24 gold seekers, 18 returned to town. Five were never seen again.

The body of Reds, the instigator, was seen a week later, floating in the creek, his neck broken. Probably from a fall during the confusion, some said. Others weren't so sure.

Trespassing fell off quite a bit after what is still referred to as the Great Treasure Hunt in the Wedge.

No one wanted to cross with Melinda.

But some still wondered how she could have lived so long. It was nearly 100 years since the Civil War when the stories began.

Did the herbs and berries of the forest contribute to her long life?

Was there a coven of witches in the woods and the original Melinda dead, a new one in her place?

Was it the magical powers of the witch that enabled her to exist forever?

No one could determine the answer.

"Who cares why?" said the old folk. "Why do you newcomers need an answer for everything? Just let things be."

Made sense, and people did.

In the early 1950s, however, people began moving to the suburbs where housing developments offered all the conveniences of town in your own little piece of the country.

Mr. Salvatore, a well-known developer with wavy dark hair and an extra wide smile, came over from Wilmington. He bought up a big chunk of The Wedge and announced plans to put in about 250 homes.

He didn't care about the stupid stories of Melinda the Witch. It was 1952. People were sophisticated, smart, slick and, most importantly, they had money and wanted a share of the American Dream.

He was going to give them what they desired and make himself a good amount of money in the process. While the locals shook their heads, Mr. Salvatore and his crew headed out along Hopkins Road and chopped down a clearing.

Arriving with surveying instruments and construction equipment, they staked out the area with red and white tape and drove freshly cut wooden stakes into the ground.

When they came back to the site the next day, they couldn't find any of their markings. The tape and stakes were gone, the holes filled in.

Thinking local kids were being mischievous, they hammered in the stakes a second time, but deeper and harder than before.

Again, when they arrived the following morning, everything was gone.

Determined, Mr. Salvatore hired one of his crew to stay the night and guard their third attempt to mark the site where the machinery would soon begin digging up the forest.

The guard lasted until 9 o'clock and then fled.

He never came back to work, quit by phone the next day, mumbling something about being attacked by a bear.

Angry about the delay, Mr. Salvatore ordered the whole crew to stay the next night. He bought them dinner and flashlights, and the five workers sat in the truck.

Two were in the front cab. Three stayed in the back, and they took turns sleeping.

The rustling started. It was coming from the area where the stakes had been placed.

Now wide awake, all five men slowly entered the woods. Three with flashlights, two holding large shovels for protection.

The stakes were gone. But, in each of the dozen spots where they had been, was an animal, an amazingly large raccoon with glowing red eyes, razor sharp teeth and a mouth dripping with white foam.

In a flash, the dark striped, snarling animals charged for the workmen, who dropped whatever they were holding and ran as fast as they could for the truck.

But, it was gone.

It wasn't there.

They saw it heading, at full speed, straight for a gigantic tree.

In shock, the workers shook as the truck smashed head-on into the base of a large tree.

They waited at the roadside until morning. When their boss arrived, they demanded a ride back to Wilmington and all quit as a group.

With no crew, Mr. Salvatore decided to handle things himself. That night, he sat in his Cadillac on Hopkins Road, watching the woods, waiting for a chance to kill the Witch in The Wedge or whatever was delaying his project.

It was quiet, so very still.

He heard the rustling to his left, opened the car door, and headed slowly into the woods. A pistol was in his right hand, a flashlight in the other.

When he arrived at the clearing that he had staked by himself, he saw a dozen rabbits gnawing on the tape and digging at the dirt that held his stakes. Shinning the straight, yellow beam on one, he fired. The bullet missed its mark, but the animals disappeared into the woods.

Laughing, he found a stump and sat.

"Fools!" he said aloud. "The fools were scared off by a band of little baby bunnies!"

Immediately, a wave of heat wrapped around his body. It was so overpowering that he was filled with fear.

Without seeing anything, Mr. Salvatore knew he was being stalked, surrounded, about to be grabbed.

The unseen force was thick, black, threatening. He couldn't lift his arms, was unable to move his finger that remained frozen around the trigger of his pistol.

Whatever, whoever it was, had surrounded him tightly, pressing against his body. There was no escape. He couldn't move.

As his shoulders continued to be crushed inward—toward the center of his body, squeezing into his chest—he heard the voice.

It was shrill, high pitched but soft, sounding like the thin edge of chalk screeching against a blackboard.

"*Leave my woods, now, or you will die!*"

Although the warning was only given once, he believed the message.

As the pressure around his shoulders was released, a steady force moved downward, against the top of his head. He tried to resist, to get away, but was afraid to move. The hand, with a vise-like grip, could easily crush his skull.

Slowly, Mr. Salvatore, by this time crying like a baby, was shoved toward the ground of the forest, the claw-like pressure continued on the crown of his head until his body was flat against the dirty floor of the woods.

That's when he saw the eyes, hundreds of them, surrounding him, as the animals of the forest moved closer and closer. The last thing he recalled, before he lost consciousness, was the fear that he was going to be eaten alive.

No one saw Mr. Salvatore the next day.

His Cadillac was discovered empty, the driver's door open. People figured he headed off into the woods.

A few folks expected to see his boots on the side of the road, but not even that happened.

No one came back to put out any more stakes.

The development idea fizzled, especially when a strange man was found on Route 40, near Perryville, two weeks later.

The man was wandering the side of the highway early one morning, his clothes shredded into rags, bites all over his body. The Maryland police found his I.D. and called the troopers in Delaware.

It was Mr. Salvatore.

There was nothing in the paper, but a friend of a friend of a friend said when he was picked up, the police thought the guy had escaped from a nearby state mental hospital.

The contractor was babbling like a lunatic, telling anyone who would listen that he had been attacked by a bunch of rabbits and raccoons. The police have the interview on tape. They say it's a riot to listen to. They made copies and passed it around to their friends.

The guy can be heard saying the rabbits were going to eat him alive and an old red-eyed witch who tried to crush his skull.

But, the strangest thing of all is that Mr. Salvatore, who had a thick head of dark black hair, was never seen in public again without a hat.

You see, after that night in the woods, there appeared a bright white, thin, claw-like hand print outline in his hair. It can't be washed away and continues to grow back. It can't even be cut away.

Mr. Salvatore's is in his 70s now, but he still carries the mark of Melinda, the Witch of The Wedge. It will be with him forever.

The state now owns the preserve, bought it years ago.

There are about 2,000 acres in Delaware and Pennsylvania, and it extends into another adjacent 5,000 acres in Maryland.

It will never be developed into houses, that's for sure.

But, if you read the newspapers, there is talk in Delaware about flooding the area and using it as a reservoir, building a large dam. And in Maryland, there's been a proposal to use a portion of the public land for a golf course.

I don't think Melinda would like either of those ideas.

Do you?

The Easter Gathering

Brenda Porcelli was desperately in need of a new apartment, but the classified ad in the *Clef*, the student newspaper of Baltimore's Alfred Mannus Music University, sounded too good to be true.

> Apt. for rent: Within walking distance of campus. Utilities included. SINGLE FEMALES ONLY. No males. No couples. No calls. Apply in person. 666 DeParte Circle N.W. Ask for Miss Gritts. $150 a month.

As she ripped out the ad, Brenda reflected on her three hectic weeks of apartment hunting that had brought no satisfactory results. Using her newly acquired rental-searching knowledge, she knew the housing was in a good neighborhood. Therefore, the listing fell into three possible categories: a come-on, a misprint or a miracle meant to be.

Hoping for a heavenly gift, Brenda left the apartment she shared with a roommate who had been nothing but trouble, and headed for the nearest cab stop. She wanted to be the first one through the doors and, if everything was agreeable, the new tenant.

To Brenda, spring was the nicest time of year in Baltimore. The trees and plants were starting to reappear after hiding for months from the ice and snow of the harsh winter. The air was fresh. Although the sky was overcast, it was good to be outside again.

The wind started to blow intensely just as the cab stopped at the address.

"Are you sure this is it?" she leaned forward and asked the driver.

"Hey, lady, this is the address you gave me. Look, up there on the plaque!"

His hand pointed to the bronze metal plate, attached to a tall, stone post. It read:

CHANDLER L. DePARTE
MORTUARY and CREMATORIUM
666 DeParte Circle N.W.

Shaking her head, Brenda paid the cabbie and stepped out onto the pavement. A sudden gust of wind threw dust into her eye. Dabbing the tears with a handkerchief, she tried to focus on the imposing structure. In the distance was a massive three-story, 19th-century mansion with large, ornately carved, double doors that held thick panes of multi-colored stained glass.

There were several turrets and bay windows, quite a few gables, a gray slate roof and, of course, dozens of small, threatening gargoyles that were frozen like permanent guards.

Passing through the iron gate, which was slightly ajar, Brenda followed the brick walkway that led toward the main door. A meticulous garden with several goldfish ponds presented a country-like setting in the middle of the city. The entire compound was enclosed by a 10-foot-high wall. Sharp shards of broken glass were embedded in the top flat section of the barrier. They had been placed there to threaten intruders and impress visitors.

Before Brenda could organize her thoughts and sort out the questions forming in her mind, the front door opened slowly.

"I'm Miss Gritts," said the stiff, humorless greeting party of one. "Please follow me," the sentinel commanded and Brenda automatically obeyed.

Walking through the mansion gave Brenda a chill. She had always hated funeral parlors, ever since her father had forced her to kiss grandmother good-bye as her lifeless form lay in the coffin.

Even though the incident had occurred 15 years before, Brenda, now 20, could still recall the cold roughness of dear departed Gran Gran's dark, red painted lips.

But, on this spring day curiosity and basic economics helped the practical college student overcome silly childhood fears. Miss Gritts, about 50 and well preserved, walked with a crisp, businesslike gait; her footsteps echoed across the building's polished marble floor.

As they entered the main office, which was carpeted and plush, Brenda was introduced to Chandler DeParte, the owner. He was a frail but feisty 69-year-old entrepreneur with a thin, chalky gray face. On the top of his cane rested two bony claws, which, at times, he rubbed together, reminding Brenda of a Boy Scout trying to start a fire with two thin sticks.

Next in line was Roland, Chandler's younger, 65-year-old brother. He was five times the size of the patriarch and, what Chandler left on his dinner plate Roland obviously polished off. At 5 foot 7 inches, and weighing in at no less than 250 pounds, Roland reminded Brenda of a very well-fed and bloated human tick.

At the far end of the room, in the shadows and seated on a Victorian-style chaise lounge, was Roland's wife, Mrs. Cassandra DeParte. Like Miss Gritts, the middle-aged socialite appeared fit and stern. With her red and black gown and heavy gold jewelry, Dame Cassandra DeParte looked like someone who could either tell your fortune or do a decent job on your hair and nails.

No one rose or spoke any greeting. Only condescending nods were offered and Miss Gritts, standing between Brenda and the jury, broke the silence.

Speaking crisply, with her hands clasped at the front of her waist, she began: "Miss Porcelli, the DePartes are very interested in knowing all they can about their future tenant. Therefore, it is necessary that you answer a number of questions. If your responses are satisfactory, you will be shown the facilities and offered an opportunity to reside here."

Brenda nodded and forced a smile. Immediately, the questions came in rapid, staccato fashion from the family. The queries came so quickly that Brenda had to concentrate to keep track of the initiators. Eventually, she ended up responding to the group.

"How old are you, dear?" asked Mrs. DeParte.

"Almost 21."

"Why do you want the apartment?" said Roland.

"I want to live on my own. I'm tired of roommates and their problems that always seem to become mine."

"Anything else?" Mrs. DeParte pressed.

I'm a music major, an organist. This location is closer to my classes. Since I have to practice at school a lot, and perform in quite a few recitals, your apartment would be id . . . "

"Where do you live now?" someone asked.

"All the way over in Dundalk."

"Do you have any close friends?" another person queried.

"No."

"A boyfriend then?"

"No."

"Why not? You seem to be an attractive young thing," said Roland, licking his lips and staring at Brenda.

"Because I'm too involved in my music, and I don't have time for any of that!" Brenda snapped, her tone indicated she was becoming upset.

"We will not permit you to bring young men into your apartment and entertain," stressed Mrs. DeParte.

"That's not a problem, as I've already explained, I don't have any time for . . . . "

"Where were you born?" asked Roland.

"California."

"Does your family live there?"

"I have no family. My parents died in a car crash when I was 9, and I lived in several state-supervised foster homes."

"How will you pay the rent? Where does your money come from?" asked Chandler in a thin, high-pitched voice.

"I think that's a personal question, and I don't think it's any of your business!" said Brenda, not bothering to hide her aggravation and obviously upset with the interrogation.

Sensing the young girl's annoyance, Miss Gritts intervened.

"Miss Porcelli, please don't take these questions personally. We are simply trying to make sure that you are responsible and serious enough to be considered for our apartment. I'm sure you realize that these questions are the same type that would be asked on any written rental application.

"Most of them," Brenda said, nodding. But she began to relax and Miss Gritts continued the questioning.

"Now, just a few more insignificant questions: What is your date of birth?"

"December 6, 1974.

"And your blood type?" interjected Chandler.

""B Positive. Why?"

"Just curious. I have a theory about birthdates and blood types," he explained casually.

"You are Italian?" Mrs. DeParte asked.

"American," Brenda snapped. "But, the records state that both my parents were of Italian descent. My father, Antoine Porcelli, came to this country from Italy after World War II."

Tapping his cane against the edge of the thick table nearby, Chandler signaled to Miss Gritts that the interview was finished.

"You seem to have satisfied the DePartes," she said to Brenda. "They would like me to show you the apartment."

Forced smiles were flashed at Brenda by her three inquisitors.

Again following Miss Gritts, Brenda passed through a hallway flanked by four large parlors. Antiques, velvet curtains, ornate mirrors and overstuffed chairs were scattered throughout the building. Miss Gritts opened a solid black walnut door that led into a narrow circular stairway. Holding onto the rail, Brenda ascended to the second floor that opened into a long narrow hall.

A single door stood at the far end. Unlocking it, Miss Gritts motioned for Brenda to enter.

The college student was shocked by the mini-palace before her eyes. A sitting room was connected to a modern eat-in kitchen with a stove, microwave and full-sized refrigerator. A private, full bath—with shower—was off the bedroom.

Since the mansion had been constructed during the last century, the rooms were very large, and two stained glass windows overlooked the gardens and street below. Brenda could see the Charm City skyline in the distance. The view was fantastic.

"There is a private entrance from the garden area and a parking site if you have a vehicle," Miss Gritts said. "But, I was told to mention that there was a mistake regarding the price in the advertisement."

Here it comes, thought Brenda.

"The DePartes will rent this apartment to you for $110 a month. Also, you may have noticed a large organ—which once was used in a Baltimore city movie house—in the first floor of the Home. They will allow you to practice on it if you wish. Now, do you have any questions?"

"You mean, I can have the apartment?"

"Yes. If you find the terms agreeable."

"What are they?"

"Only one. No men in these rooms—ever! The DePartes would become furious if that occurred and evict you immediately. Is that understood?"

"Yes. As I said, that is not a problem."

"Very well. There is no written lease. Either side can terminate at will with five days' notice. However, I'm sure you will find the Home very agreeable."

"I'm sure," Brenda agreed. "Let me ask you something. Why is this place so cheap?"

"Money is of no consequence to the DePartes. They only are interested in ensuring that the proper type of person lives in the Home. Such an individual has been difficult to discover. You are quite fortunate to have met their strict standards and you should consider yourself both fortunate and flattered." Pausing, Miss Gritts narrowed her eyes and focused intently on Brenda, "So, can I tell them you will be taking the apartment?"

"Yes! Definitely," Brenda said, smiling and offering her hand to Miss Gritts.

Responding with a firm but cold shake, the officious guide asked, "When will you be moving in?"

"By the end of the week."

"Good. I'm sure the DePartes will be pleased. Welcome to the Home."

❋   ❋   ❋   ❋

Brenda's first week in her new apartment was fantastic. With no need to catch the bus to class, she was able to sleep an hour longer every morning. But her real pleasure was playing the Home's theater organ. It was in excellent condition and saved her numerous trips to the campus.

The DePartes seemed to enjoy her music. Often, Roland's wife and Chandler would sit nearby, in overstuffed chairs, never speaking, just watching and listening. Initially, Brenda was distracted, but she became comfortable with their presence.

At the end of her second week, in mid-March, the dream began. The first time, she was shaken. The second time it was so vivid, she actually screamed herself awake.

As the dream continued to occur, on alternate nights, she tried to figure out what it meant. The more she thought, the more she worried.

Each dream was essentially the same. Brenda saw herself at a party, wearing a long black gown. The setting seemed familiar. Everyone was smiling. Most were older, and they were raising tiny glasses. Toasting someone, something at the celebration.

There was a bright red, glowing light, and one younger man. He was handsome with dark hair and hypnotic eyes. Big, black eyes. He seemed to be very close to her, so close. His eyes were deep, shiny. Sparkling. She was lying down. On satin. It was so hot. Then, the gathering of people all started shouting . . . words in unison. But she couldn't make them out. "Ma . . . ! Vi . . . ! Del . . . !"

Then she would awaken.

She mentioned it to a friend at school who had an undergraduate degree in psychology. They agreed that it was just a fluke. Nothing to worry about. Her dream was probably a manifestation of some inner anxiety which she had suppressed during her conscious hours. Sleep provided an opportunity to release tension and the dream was the vehicle which Brenda subconsciously used. Besides, the friend added, "Don't you think the fact that you're living in a funeral parlor might have a tendency to heighten your level of uneasiness just a bit?"

They both laughed, and few days later Brenda's dream stopped.

✳   ✳   ✳   ✳

Easter always arrived more suddenly than Christmas. Maybe it was because it wasn't on the same date each year and you could never be positive of which Sunday it would be until it was very close. Therefore, Brenda had two surprises when Miss Gritts approached one afternoon at the Home's organ. It was the Monday before Easter, and Brenda was informed that the DePartes wanted her to perform at a Gathering on Saturday night.

"The family has been pleased with your living habits and impressed by your musical talent."

Brenda was amazed since her landlords hadn't spoken two words to her since she had arrived nearly a month ago.

"Well, it's such short notice . . .. "

"I know it's a bit late," Miss Gritts agreed, "but you should be flattered that the DePartes think so highly of you. Unless you have a major commitment," she continued, sternly, "it would only be common courtesy for you to agree. After all, they have given you an excellent apartment at a fraction of its real worth. Plus, I will add, you certainly have taken full advantage of your organ privileges."

Brenda was beginning to feel guilty.

"Do they have any preference as to what I should play?"

The stern messenger smiled broadly and handed Brenda the music.

94

"The *Mephisto Waltz*? That isn't an organ piece. To be performed properly, it should be played on a piano. And it's not the easiest selection to prepare in less than a week's time. Plus, I don't think it's appropriate for an Easter party."

Annoyed by Brenda's comments, Miss Gritts cut in, "The DePartes and their guests will not care whether it is performed on the piano, organ or harmonica. It is to be thought of as a ceremonial piece, actually, the centerpiece of the evening program. A surprise for one of the guests. Also, this is not to be considered an 'Easter' party. We do not use the term 'Easter' in the Home, for it may offend some of the influential guests. Think of it as the Home's annual springtime Gathering.

"Finally, they have instructed me to give you this $500 check for your services."

"I don't want any money. I'll be glad to play for . . . . "

"The DePartes believe one does his or her best when all arrangements are maintained at a professional level," Miss Gritts snapped. "If you were to use their services, they would expect to be paid, for they, too, are recognized professionals. You, young lady, should be flattered that they think of you the same way. The Gathering will begin at 10 o'clock. You will be present at that time, even though you will perform later in the evening. The attire, naturally, is formal. What do you wear when you perform?"

"A long black skirt and top," Brenda replied.

"Excellent. That will be quite appropriate. Also, display no jewelry, please."

"Why?"

"It's just one of the rules. Any other questions?"

Brenda shook her head.

"Good. We shall see you Saturday. Be sure to be on time. You don't have far to travel."

"Tell the DePartes I appreciate their confidence in me and I'll do the best I can."

"I'm sure you will, my dear. Keep in mind, the people attending the gathering are very influential. Who knows what valuable contact you will make? Oh, and one final item, please don't tell anyone, at school or anywhere else, about the event. It's to be a surprise for the guest of honor, and we don't want word to slip out. Baltimore is still a small town among the upper levels of society. It would be a disaster if the surprise were to be spoiled."

"Well, you don't have to worry. I don't know anyone important."

"Still," Miss Gritts stressed, "no one is to know. This is a very private, secret affair."

"All right. No problem."

As Miss Gritts' footsteps echoed off the hallway floor, Brenda began to practice Liszt's *Mephisto Waltz*. With nothing to do on Saturday night and no special plans for Easter, the party would help kill another typically dull weekend.

❊   ❊   ❊   ❊

The Home's foyer was jammed with people, and the adjoining viewing parlors were beginning to fill. Everyone was well dressed—the men in tuxedos, the women in designer evening gowns. At the entrance, the DePartes stood bedecked in their finery and greeted those arriving.

As soon as she appeared, Brenda was escorted by Miss Gritts to her landlords, who placed the young organist in the receiving line between Roland and Chandler.

"You look beautiful this evening, my dear. Doesn't she, Roland?" remarked Chandler.

"Yes, ravishing," he replied, licking his lips with a fat tongue that looked like a glob of pink modeling clay.

"Stay with us and greet our friends, dear," ordered Mrs. DeParte, who wore a black silk skirt and a matching top trimmed in red.

By 10:30, the incoming flow had subsided. Mrs. DeParte took Brenda's arm and introduced her to the most important guests. Although she did not recognize any of their names, some of the faces looked familiar. Brenda actually thought she had seen some of them in old movies and books.

The DePartes had assured their young guest that only those who had made it to the top were at The Gathering in the Home. Networking, they said, would be in high gear tonight.

Interestingly, Brenda was asked the same questions by nearly every one she met—her nationality, age, where she was born and if she had any boyfriends.

Mrs. DeParte brushed away Brenda's concerns, explaining that older people had no experience speaking to the young and they often were at a loss for words. The questions were superficial, cocktail party banter. Pay no attention.

Brenda felt she was being pacified by her escort's explanation, but she did agree with one thing—all the guests were old. There were few attending the event who were under 60.

Creeping over, with his walking stick tapping away, was Chandler, who cut a distinguished figure in his tuxedo. "Is our little pet ready to perform?" he cackled. With one claw resting on his cane, he placed the other on Brenda's shoulder.

"Yes, Mr. DeParte. Whenever you're ready."

"Well, let's say in about five minutes, dear. And, by the way, you are the talk of the gathering, my lovely. They all want to know where I discovered you. Imagine what they'll think after they hear you play. Every single one of them will just be drooling with envy."

After a brief introduction, Brenda nodded to the audience and took her seat at the organ. Because the instrument was in the foyer, only the most important guests were able to have seats where they could see the performance. The rest were able to listen from their places in the adjoining parlors.

The DePartes and Miss Gritts sat in the front row. There was a slightly elevated, empty throne-like chair between Chandler and Roland.

Brenda attacked the waltz with passion. She had practiced the entire week, day and night, and she felt well prepared. Even as she approached the most difficult passages her anticipated apprehension never surfaced. It was as if some force, some power, was driving her to play faster, stronger and better than she had ever done before. She performed as is she were auditioning for an important role, her opportunity of a lifetime.

She felt the perspiration on her forehead. Her arms and fingers ached. But she pushed aside the pain. In its place, she substituted the pages she had memorized during the last five days and nights.

She was the best that evening. She would show them all. They would be pleased. Proud. Excited! After she touched the final chord, she rested her hands on her lap, lowered her head, and there was silence.

A moment later, as she turned to face the audience, screams of approval, rounds of applause and delightful accolades roared through the Home. They were on their feet, clapping. Smiling.

All except one.

He occupied the throne.

He was young and handsome and wore a tuxedo. Brenda rose to bow, but her eyes were locked on his.

Chandler hobbled over to the organ and called for quiet. Miss Gritts and Roland also motioned to the crowd, which responded slowly.

When absolute silence had returned, Chandler spoke. "My dear, you are excellent. Much better than we could have hoped for. It's been many, many years since we have experienced someone so young with your grace and talent in the Home."

Again, applause rose from the gathering. Tapping his cane, he one more signaled for quiet. "My pet, our guest of honor, Baron Zantanski would like to present you with a gift. Consider it a small token of our appreciation."

The Baron, the handsome young man in the tuxedo rose. For the first time, Brenda saw the graceful black cape that flowed behind him. In his hand, he held a black velvet bag. Placing his white-gloved inside, he withdrew a long, golden necklace, from which dangled a glowing red stone the size of a silver dollar.

Holding the clasps of the chain, he approached Brenda and placed his hands around her throat. As he attached the clasp, the glowing red ember rested on her breast.

The crowd applauded. Facing the audience, he announced in a slight Slavic accent, "And now a toast to the beautiful, young fair Maiden!"

"To our Maiden!" he bellowed.

"To our Maiden!" repeated the guests of the gathering.

"And now, my dear," said the Baron, taking her arm and handing her a fine, crystal glass, "If you would be so kind to join me in a private toast."

As the ornate goblets touched, Brenda's eyes again locked on the Baron's. She tossed back her head and quickly downed her champagne.

For an indeterminate amount of time, Brenda walked beside the guest of honor. Then, for some reason, she began to falter, to stumble. He pulled her closer and easily supported her weight. Even so, her arms grew weak and Brenda began to feel sleepy.

"I'm sorry," she said. "I don't know why I'm so weak. If I could just lie down for a moment."

"Of course," the Baron replied as he lifted her into his arms and carried her across the room. As he passed the grandfather clock outside the main parlor, he noticed it was one minute before midnight.

Then she saw the Baron's eyes. Dark. Black. Handsome eyes. As he placed her on a bed lined in soft, red satin, the ember dangling from the necklace seemed to be burning. She could feel it against her breast. It was so warm. So hot. But she couldn't move her arms. They were like lead weights, immovable at her sides.

At midnight the hands of the clock meshed. As they did every 12 hours, the chimes tolled, their single tones echoed through the Home.

One!

Brenda felt so light. So helpless.

Two!

The Baron smiled over her. His presence was hypnotic.

Three!

His teeth glistened. Sharp. Long. Pointed.

Four!

His face came close. His breath was hot.

Five!

She heard the shouts. "Maiden! Maiden!" Hot breath warmed her neck.

Six!

His teeth were at her throat. She felt a pinch. A snap. The crowd shouted again, "Virgin! Virgin!"

Seven!

They raised glasses. Small empty glasses. A hose, a thin, clear tube, was near her neck.

Eight!

She had no strength to lift her hand, to push it away. "Maiden! Virgin!"

Nine!

She was close to unconsciousness. Some of them were standing over her. Their glasses were full now—full of dark, hot wine.

Ten!

Lips were stained. The red color was wet, glistened. Roland emptied his glass. He licked his lips and cried, "Excellent!"

Eleven!

Blackness.

Twelve!

"Delicious!" they repeated again and again.

"Delicious!" they nodded and agreed.

Chandler stood arm and arm with the Baron, looking down

from their perch at the edge of the coffin. They congratulated themselves as the guests lined up, holding glasses, waiting for their portion of the Maiden.

* * * *

Baron Zantanski was the last to leave at four in the morning, well before sunrise. Rather than being tired, the DePartes and Miss Gritts were too excited to sleep.

"A fine Gathering, Chandler!" said Mrs. DeParte, smiling, and offering him a toast.

"Yes, it was, my dear. And she was an excellent feature, that young pet. I always said California raises a good crop."

"And," Roland added, "1974 was, without a doubt, a very good year."

"The Baron was very impressed," Miss Gritts said. "He told me to inform you that he is very pleased with the way you handle your Gatherings. And he definitely will return for your Winterfest this December."

"Tremendous!" cackled Chandler, tapping his cane with delight. "The Baron, above all, should appreciate how difficult it is to come up with a virgin in this day and age."

"But you seem to succeed every time," Roland said.

"Yes," Chandler sighed, "but it will be very hard to top Brenda. She was, without exception, the best we have ever had at the Home. Don't you agree, Cassandra?"

"Absolutely, Chandler. She was a Gathering's dream. Talented. Beautiful. Polite, and indescribably delicious. When will you begin to advertise for the Winterfest Maiden?"

"In light of last night's success, I believe we should begin sooner than usual. Traditionally, we start in September with the opening of the college season, but this year we'll move it up by a month, to August. Competition is becoming very keen, and we don't want the Baron going elsewhere. Heaven knows who they might send in his place."

"An excellent idea, Chandler," said Mrs. DeParte. "Now, we have a little surprise for you."

On his wife's nod, Roland produced a small decanter from under his tuxedo jacket and handed it to Chandler. The printed label stated:

Porcelli of California
1974
'A *very good year*'

"Oh, how delightful," cooed Chandler, tapping his cane in glee and pressing the cut glass container against his thin, gray lips. "You shouldn't have. But, then again . . . . Mmmm!"

"Well," sang Miss Gritts, in a smooth, slow, cocktail lounge style, "It's a long, long time . . . from March to December."

Author's note: Brenda Porcelli is still listed as missing in official records. Her disappearance has not been solved and attempts to convince law enforcement officials to pursue leads related to strange activities at the DeParte Mortuary and Crematorium have not been successful. Perhaps the publication of this story will help complete this ongoing investigation.

About the Author

Ed Okonowicz, a Delaware native and freelance writer, is an editor and writer at the University of Delaware, where he earned a bachelor's degree in music education and a master's degree in communication.

Also a professional storyteller, Ed is a member of the National Storytelling Association. He presents programs at country inns, retirement homes, schools, libraries, private *gatherings*, public events. Elderhostels and theaters in the mid-Atlantic region.

He specializes in local legends and folklore of the Delaware and Chesapeake Bays, as well as topics related to the Eastern Shore of Maryland. He also writes and tells city stories, many based on his youth growing up in his family's beer garden–Adolph's Cafe–in the Browntown section of Wilmington, Delaware.

Ed presents storytelling courses and writing workshops based on his book *How to Conduct an Interview and Write an Original Story*. With his wife, Kathleen, they present a popular workshop entitled, *Self Publishing: All You Need to Know about Getting—or Not Getting—into the Business*.

About the Artist

Kathleen Burgoon Okonowicz, a watercolor artist and illustrator, is originally from Greenbelt, Maryland. She studied art in high school and college, and began focusing on realism and detail more recently under Geraldine McKeown. She enjoys taking things of the past and preserving them in her paintings.

Her first full-color, limited-edition print, *Special Places*, was released in January 1995. The painting features a stately stairway near the Brandywine River in Wilmington, Delaware.

A graduate of Salisbury State University, Kathleen earned her master's degree in professional writing from Towson State University. She is currently a marketing specialist at the International Reading Association in Newark, Delaware.

The couple resides in Fair Hill, Maryland.

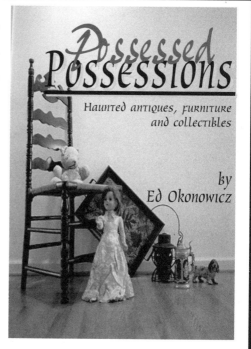

"If you're looking for an unusual gift for a collector of antiques, or enjoy haunting tales, this one's for you."
—COLLECTOR EDITIONS

" a book that will be a favorite among collectors, dealers, and fans of the supernatural alike."
—THE MIDATLANTIC ANTIQUES

". . . an intriguing read."
—MAINE ANTIQUE DIGEST

". . . a good way to relax following a long day walking an antique show or waiting at an auction. The book is certainly entertaining, and it's even a bit disturbing.
—ANTIQUEWEEK

A bump. A thud. Mysterious movement. Unexplained happenings. Caused by what? Venture beyond the Delmarva Peninsula and discover the answer. Experience 20 eerie, true tales, plus one horrifying fictional story, about items from across the country that, apparently, have taken on an independent **spirit** of their own–for they refuse to give up the ghost.

From Maine to Florida, from Pennsylvania to Wisconsin . . . haunted heirlooms exist among us . . . everywhere.

Read about them in **Possessed Possessions**, *the book some antique dealers definitely do not want you to buy.*

$9.95

112 pages
5 1/2 x 8 1/2 inches
softcover
ISBN 0-9643244-5-8

Currently In Progress

MORE *Possessed* Possessions*2*
Haunted Antiques, Furniture and Collectibles

Volume I
Pulling Back the Curtain

The first book in a series of true ghost stories. Relive 8 real-life ghostly experiences and enjoy 2 local legends.

"A treat from professional storyteller Okonowicz."

Invisible Ink
ghost catalog

$8.95

64 pages   5 1/2 x 8 1/2 inches   softcover   ISBN 0-9643244-0-7

Volume II
Opening the Door

13 more true-life Delmarva ghost tales and one peninsula legend are sure to keep you up at night.

" 'Scary' Ed Okonowicz . . . the master of written fear— at least on the Delmarva Peninsula . . . has done it again."

Wilmington News Journal

$8.95

96 pages   5 1/2 x 8 1/2 inches   softcover   ISBN 0-9643244-3-1

Volume III
Welcome Inn

Features true stories of unusual events in haunted inns, restaurants, and museums and includes "Concert by Candlelight," winner of a 1996 Storytelling World Honor Award.

". . . a sort of auto-club guide to ghosts, spirits and the unexplainable . . . ."

Theresa Humphrey, Associated Press

$8.95

96 pages   5 1/2 x 8 1/2 inches   softcover   ISBN 0-9643244-4-X

Get yourself into the *Spirits* ...

To collect all the volumes, or to be a part of the next book, complete the form below:

Name _____

Address _____

City _____ State _____ Zip Code _____

Phone Numbers ( ) _____ Day   ( ) _____ Evening

_____ I would like to be placed on the mailing list to receive the free *Spirits Speaks* newsletter and information on future volumes.

_____ I have an experience I would like to share. Please call me. (Each person who sends in a submission will be contacted. If your story is used, you will receive a free copy of the volume in which your experience appears.)

I would like to order the following books:

Quantity	Title	Price	Total
	Possessed Possessions	$9.95	
	Pulling Back the Curtain, Vol. I	$8.95	
	Opening the Door, Vol. II	$8.95	
	Welcome Inn, Vol. III	$8.95	
	In the Vestibule, Vol. IV	$9.95	
	Presence in the Parlor, Vol. V	$9.95	
	Stairway over the Brandywine	$5.00	

*MD residents add 5% sales tax.

Subtotal _____

Please include $1.50 postage for first book, and 50 cents for each additional book.

Tax* _____

Shipping _____

Total _____

All books are signed by the author. If you would like the book(s) personalized, please specify to whom.

Mail to: Ed Okonowicz
             1386 Fair Hill Lane
             Elkton, MD 21921

Make checks payable to: Myst and Lace Publishers, Inc.